# DANCE of the DARK HEART

Other books by JULIE HEARN

# Julie Hearn

## DANCE of the DARK HEART

**OXFORD**
UNIVERSITY PRESS

# OXFORD
UNIVERSITY PRESS

Great Clarendon Street, Oxford OX2 6DP

Oxford University Press is a department of the University of Oxford.
It furthers the University's objective of excellence in research, scholarship,
and education by publishing worldwide in

Oxford   New York

Auckland   Cape Town   Dar es Salaam   Hong Kong   Karachi
Kuala Lumpur   Madrid   Melbourne   Mexico City   Nairobi
New Delhi   Shanghai   Taipei   Toronto

With offices in

Argentina   Austria   Brazil   Chile   Czech Republic   France   Greece
Guatemala   Hungary   Italy   Japan   Poland   Portugal   Singapore
South Korea   Switzerland   Thailand   Turkey   Ukraine   Vietnam

Oxford is a registered trade mark of Oxford University Press
in the UK and in certain other countries

British Library Cataloguing in Publication Data
Data available

ISBN: 978-0-19-272930-9

1 3 5 7 9 10 8 6 4 2

Printed in Great Britain

Paper used in  the production of this book is a natural,
recyclable product made from wood grown in sustainable forests.
The manufacturing process conforms to the environmental
regulations of the country of origin.

*For my nephew and nieces,*
*Matthew, Elise, Jessica and Kerry Hearn.*

Jack Orion was as good a fiddler
As ever fiddled on a string
And he could make young women mad
With the tune his wires would sing

*Jack Orion* (Trad.)


'. . . it makes my heart die to think what fortune I
have that I cannot be always in your company.'

*Letter to Thomas Culpeper from*
*Katherine Howard, Queen of England, Spring 1541*

# I

There had been omens. Bad ones. A blood-coloured ring around the moon. Crows on the woodpile, watching the shack. A tree that fell without being axed, keeling over in its prime, like a man with a curse on him.

Old Scratch noted these occurrences—the moon, the crows, the tree—but kept his own counsel. For one thing, he had no one to tell. For another, nature had sent him trouble enough, that winter, without him seeing more of it wherever he happened to look.

The snow had come early, blanketing the land on All Souls' Eve and re-covering it at regular intervals, up to and beyond the Solstice. Old Scratch had never known such a persistent piling up of the stuff. Day in, day out it came, with drifts touching what passed for his roof and no respite, not even on melt days, because the melting only went so far before the sky turned goosey-grey again and down came another load, white upon white upon white.

Old Scratch was sick of the sight of so much white. It pained his eyes. It gave him bad dreams in which he went wading, thigh-deep, through rivers of milk, or unravelled a shroud, layer after bone-white layer, terrified of who, or what, he might uncover.

Even his goats were white, the lumpen things, and getting to them—keeping a path clear, from his shack to theirs—was griping his back and doing little to improve a temper that had never been all that sunny.

Although not yet ancient, or even especially old, years of scraping along with no one to share a sup of ale with, or a cuddle, or a laugh, had taken their toll on Scratch. He was as dry as a stick. As reclusive as a snail. And extreme weather conditions jangled him, the way extreme emotions might have done, had he ever been exposed to any.

When the knock came, at what passed for his door, his heart leapt so high, and banged so fast that he put a hand to his chest and pressed it there, as if to keep things in.

It was late afternoon, January twelfth, the sky and the snow such a similar shade of nothing-at-all that the world beyond the shack seemed to be in limbo, with no up or down to it and no way in or out.

There had been a melt that day, but not enough—nowhere near enough, Old Scratch was certain—to allow for easy walking, and only a fool would have risked laming a horse along lanes as slippy as glass.

'Who's there?' His voice sounded odd, so he cleared his throat and tried again. It had been three moons, at least, he realized, since he had spoken to another living soul.

'Is it you, young Frizzle Face? Is it?'

No answer came, but then it wouldn't.

'Bang thrice more if it be thee. Four times if you have something I'd like and would fain come in.'

Silence.

Old Scratch scowled and scratched at his rags.

'Bothersome boy,' he muttered, lurching the few steps to where his door sagged against an impediment of logs. 'Tiresome little whelp.'

But his mouth watered as he began tossing aside the logs, for the boy from the monastery (who else would it be?) might have brought him an egg. Two eggs if he was lucky. Already, with another dozen or so logs still to be shifted, Old Scratch was imagining those eggs, cracked into a dish, the yolks as bright as slipping suns, the colour as welcome to him as nourishment.

'Trust you, Frizzle. Trust you to show up when I'm finished for the day, and barricaded in . . . Just like a monkery-boy to pay a call on Old Scratch when it suits the tolling of his own bell, and never mind the . . . *Sprites and fires!*'

The door fell in. Old Scratch would have caught it, normally. But this . . . these . . . what he saw . . . took him so much by surprise that he allowed the door to land, with one almighty bang, dislodging the displaced logs, and sending them tumbling, wood upon wood upon wood.

*'What in the name of all the . . . ?'*

3

# II

*I see*, the girl thought, surveying the inside of the shack and finding it no more enticing than its mean, snow-covered exterior. *I understand. I'm to give birth on a log pile, am I, with a peasant looking on? Well, if that is to be my punishment—or part of it— then so be it. I will lie among those logs as if they were the softest pillows, fat with swansdown and scented with lavender buds . . . And I will imagine this old dolt a ministering angel. I can do that. I must. I have no choice.*

She clutched at her belly, as a pain took her, and bit down, hard, on her lower lip. However much it hurt (and this first twinge had almost floored her) she had vowed to birth this . . . this . . . infant in absolute silence, partly as a penance, but mostly because she was a prideful, stubborn girl, outraged by her condition and determined to remain detached from it, even now. Especially now.

The man at her side flinched, in perfect time with her pain but without a shred of sympathy. He was older than her, by at least ten years, and if he was anything other than chilled to the bone, and severely inconvenienced, he wasn't showing it. 'Forgive us,' he said to Old Scratch. 'For startling you so. It is Goodwife Huckle we seek. I have payment.'

His voice was cultured. So was his cloak, not to mention the conker-coloured boots keeping ice and wet from his toes. Old Scratch did not doubt for one moment that this man—this stranger—had a nice weighty purse somewhere about his person. But how, in the name of all that was sacred, had he come to be standing here? And with a girl in tow, so huge with child that her belly had entered the shack ahead of her, obtuse and uninvited? What were they doing so far from high-born company, thick walls and good fires? *And how had they got through the snow?*

'There is no goodwife here.'

The girl scowled and stamped her foot, almost toppling from the effort—from the way it threw her off balance. 'I knew it,' she cried out. 'I told you, Daniel. That boy at the monastery lied to us. He guessed—didn't I tell you that he'd guessed? He sent us the wrong way on purpose, hoping, no doubt, that I would slip, and that my . . . this . . .'

'Hush!'

'No!' The girl's teeth began to chatter, but from fury, not the cold.

'Don't t-tell me to hush. It's the t-truth. You know it, as well as I.' *She's a fiery one*, Old Scratch thought. *There's bad blood there—gipsy blood, by the look of her. She's all temper, talk and trouble and will have a hard time birthing that brat of hers, unless she softens herself up and calms down.*

'Goodwife Huckle lives away towards the lake,' he said, addressing himself to the man. 'You go back to the monastery and continue on. It's two hour's walk from here.' He eyed the girl's stomach. 'Maybe three . . .' then looked over her head at the sky; darkening now, and big with snow. 'Or even four . . .'

'I'm going nowhere else today,' the girl insisted. 'Do you hear me, Daniel? Nowhere.' Shivering in earnest now, she pulled her cloak tighter around her shoulders, clutching its folds to her breast but making no effort whatsoever to cover, or warm, the lightly-clad bump that was her unborn child.

*If she were mine,* thought Scratch, *I would bridle her. I would pepper her tongue with mustard, the chit, until she learned to keep it still.*

'Please yourself,' he said, with a shrug. 'But there is no help for you here, and this cold is nipping my bones. I must attend to my barricade. Good evening to you.'

'Wait!'

The man—Daniel—put one foot over the threshold, to keep the door, such as it was, from being flung up in his face. Then he felt beneath his shirt and pulled out a purse as fat as a heart. 'Here.' he said, shaking three silver coins onto his palm and offering them, grandly, to Old Scratch. 'Take these. In exchange for shelter, and what sustenance you can spare.'

Old Scratch looked at the coins, then away, then back again. He was careful to appear disdainful, as if the deal was nothing to sing about. As if he had three times that amount of money already, banked in a secret vault, or hidden up what passed for his chimney, just waiting to be spent one day, on fripperies, or ale, or whatever else might take his fancy. A new door, perhaps, which he would think twice about opening in future to any old passer-by.

'Come away Daniel,' The girl tugged, hard, at the man's cloak. 'There is no shelter for us here. This *person* would sooner we slept in a ditch this bitter night, never more to wake. And right now, by Our Lady, so would I.'

'All right, all right.' As quick—quicker—than a magpie, Old Scratch snatched up the three silver coins, and buried them, like great big seeds, in the muck of his rags. 'You may bed down with my goats, in the shack along the path. There is straw in there, and shelter on three sides. Were the wind to blow keen from the east, you would feel it, I expect, but there is no wind tonight. Take this . . .' he limped across the muddy floor, kicking aside logs, and picked up a dish with a hunk of coarse bread in it . . . 'and this,' . . . followed by a small jug of milk.

'A *goat* shack . . . with only three . . .'

'Ava—be silent!' The man took the platter, and the jug, and nodded at Old Scratch, grateful for the giving of what anyone could see was the peasant's own poor meal, and probably all there was to eat in this sorry hovel.

'And you?' he said, kindly, to the old man. 'What is left for you?'

'Humph.' A grunt can say more than a thousand words. And this one said, as clear as any speech at court, that Old Scratch would sooner be the one going to bed without his supper than the one spending the whole of that night—the whole of his *life*—with an unbridled clacketty-tongued chit of a wife.

The girl scowled at the jug and glared at the platter.

'Come, then,' she bade her husband, 'but you'll have to pull me again. I'm not walking. And that straw had better be clean, and those goats as tame as kitty cats. And the wind had better not start blowing, from the east or from any other direction, because I'm telling you Daniel, I'm telling you for the last time . . .'

'Ava!' The man's face flushed, and then just as quickly cleared. 'Take these,' he said. 'Hold fast to them, while I pull. No—don't answer me back. Just do as I say, and bleat no more, otherwise it's many a mile I'll be from here, and from you, by morning.'

The girl took the platter, and the jug. Her hands, though mottled red and blue from the cold, were otherwise unblemished—a lady's hands, Old Scratch noted, unused to any toil greater than lifting a spoon to her mouth or pushing a needle through silk. She wore a ring with a stone in it, the colour of dried blood, and her nails were perfect ovals, cat-like in their sharpness.

'I'm sorry,' she said to her husband, although her face wasn't sorry at all. The man shook his head at her, in a knowing and weary way. *No you're not*, and then turned to attend to something, a few steps behind them, on the ground. Curious, Old Scratch waited until the girl, too, had turned away then he shuffled a pace or two after them and saw, through a whirl of fresh-falling snow, a wooden sledge draped with the pelts of wolves.

'Get on,' the man was telling the girl. 'And hold tight to that bread and milk.'

The sledge was as long as a coffin and as broad as a barge, with runners that curved, viciously, at both ends. There were thick ropes, and a harness, attached to the front. Old Scratch watched, discomfited, as the man heaved up the ropes and slung the wet, cumbersome-looking harness over and around his shoulders.

Slowly, heavily, the girl lowered herself onto the sledge, complaining all the while about having both hands full, and what if she should lose her balance, or be jolted on the way to the place where those smelly goats were wintering, up to their horrible fetlocks in their own foul messes, and with an icy blast blowing in, and . . .

'That way,' Old Scratch interrupted, pointing left. 'You can't miss it.'

The man was bent almost double, preparing to pull. Behind him, on her nest of ice-cold wolf skin, the girl began to settle herself, as best she could. There was a backrest, Old Scratch, noticed, and a board for the feet, both cunningly angled so that the girl could lean back if she wanted to and brace herself against any bumps or sudden swerves. It was quite a contraption, a sledge fit for a queen, and Old Scratch wondered who had fashioned it, and why, for it surely hadn't been made, especially, for a man to pull a heavily pregnant female through the worst snows in living memory . . . had it?

Something about the way the girl was balancing the jug and the platter on her belly, holding them there as if her stomach was a poor man's table, and nothing to do with her, roused in Old Scratch a flicker of sympathy for her unborn child.

'You'd better hurry,' he said. 'While the path to my goats is still clear and the dark not yet complete. And I want you gone at first light, whatever the weather. Farewell.'

The girl made no answer, only held herself as rigid as a martyr on a rack while another pain, a lot worse than the first, tore through her. *You* she thought, trembling as she called to mind the stranger she had been trying, and failing, to forget these many months: his wicked words, and worse . . . their bed of bracken fronds and violets, crushed to bitter sweetness . . . his face above hers, so handsome, so . . . triumphant. *You who beguiled me, and then vanished like smoke, come back! In whatever guise you choose, come back to me, please. For though the snow may boil and thunderbolts rain down upon my head, I would have you close, now that my time has come.*

But the stranger had chuckled as he took his leave of her; the sound belching back at her on a sudden hot breeze, and she would never see his face again except in the best, and worst, of her dreams.

Her husband raised his head, and looked Old Scratch straight in the eye.

'It isn't mine,' he said.

And Old Scratch, though he had never known betrayal, or anything remotely like it, guessed, correctly, that he didn't mean the extraordinary sledge. He meant the child.

*More fool you*, he thought, but didn't say, for the husband's tone had been defensive, and although he wore a harness, like any sorry beast, there was something noble, Old Scratch had to admit, about the way he was preparing to haul that faithless wife of his to a place of relative comfort, there to wait the night out before hauling her back, beyond the monastery, to where the midwife dwelt.

Love.

The husband was in love. He would have pulled his girl to Hell and back, or twice around the world. He would stand by her for ever; through all eternity, if he could. And Old Scratch felt something akin to envy in that deep-inside part of himself where, for more years than he cared to remember, only practical concerns about the weather, his goats, or the state of what passed for his roof, had quickened his pulse or kept him awake at night.

*Good riddance to you*, he muttered, as the husband heaved against the ropes, and the sledge began, slowly, to move. *And may you bother Old Scratch no more . . .*

A few moments longer he stood there, watching the sledge disappear into dancing snow, and the gathering dark. Then he flung his door back into its frame and repaired his barricade, piling the logs three deep and higher than the top of his own head, so that nothing and no one could get to him.

# III

They had gone. Old Scratch was sure of that. There were fresh sledge marks slicing past his shack and his platter and jug had been left on top of a stone, a few yards from his threshold.

Stamping and sliding towards his goats, Old Scratch sensed change in the air: a rise in temperature that would lead, he felt certain, to a proper melt before noon. The sky, although leaden, did not contain a blizzard, so far as he could tell. The cloud cover had a sulphurous tinge as if, somewhere behind it, the sun was struggling to be seen.

The goat shack, shrouded in snow, resembled a small hill. The fields, all around, were as white, and clean, as a rich man's linen. But as Old Scratch lurched onwards, he noticed streaks of red in the snow as if, in the rush and hurry of departure, the runners of the sledge had cut a small bird in half or decapitated a shrew.

Uneasy, but not panicking, yet, Old Scratch made his legs move faster.

'*Yip, yip, yip—good day my goatlings. Good day to you all.*'

Normally, upon hearing their master's voice, the goats would start to shuffle and to bleat, and Old Scratch would know each one by the sounds it made and know that all was well.

Today, though, only silence met his call.

He paused, panting, and scanned the snowy ground for hoof prints. Left, right and all around he looked, but, apart from the cuts made by the sledge, and those sinister red streaks, there were no other marks to be seen.

Unable to imagine thirteen full-grown bucks and does piled, dead or alive, upon the sledge, Old Scratch hastened around the perimeter of the shack and all but threw himself in through the side that stood open to the elements.

Blood. That was the first thing he saw. And more, far more, than he'd noticed outside: a trail of gouts and smears leading to a flattened patch of straw—straw so dark and wet it looked as if pitch had been spilled there.

*My goats . . . My girls and boys . . .*

He began to call out names. 'Lavender . . . Tussock . . . Sir Greybeard . . . Mollykins . . .' He used his soothing voice, the one they especially liked; the one that told them they had nothing to fear in this life . . . this field . . . this shelter . . .

An elderly buck raised its horn-heavy head and regarded Old Scratch with none of its usual fondness or curiosity. *Stay or go*, said the look in its piss-yellow eyes. *It matters not, any more.*

Quickly, Old Scratch did a head count. One...
two... three... He got to thirteen and then counted
again, just to be sure. They were all there, thanks be.
Unhurt, too by the look of them, only eerily silent and
absolutely still, like goats in a tapestry or a painting on
a wall.

*What terrible thing has happened here?*

It had to have been terrible, Old Scratch knew,
to have sent his whole herd into such deep shock.
Had the husband—that hen-pecked dolt—lost all
reason, he wondered? Had he been driven to the end
of his tether by his young wife's constant harping?
Was he capable, then, of murder? Or had the girl,
hating the shack, and more than usually incensed by
some remark or other, pulled a knife from about her
person—a gipsy blade, a silver dagger—and...?

When Tansy, queen of the herd, looked away from
him, distracted, he didn't immediately notice. And
the rasping sound her tongue made, as she began
licking at some object in the straw, raised no alarm
in him. He vaguely assumed she was chomping a
turnip and was relieved to think that she, at least,
had not lost her appetite or the urge to rummage
for food.

*Whose blood is this?* he was wondering. *His or hers?
And if there was a corpse to dispose of, where is it now?
On the sledge, bound for the lake? Outside, beneath the
snow? Or here, among my goats, only my old eyes have
yet to spot it or my feet to trip over its limbs?*

When the object being licked started to howl it took a while for Old Scratch to collect his thoughts and discount them, one by one. *Turnips don't cry*, he told himself. *And nor, come to that, does a stabbed-to-death body.*

All the goats were shifting now; shifting and stumbling away from the sound in the straw. Thirteen pairs of baleful yellow eyes followed Old Scratch as he hurried across the shack. *Deal with it*, those eyes all said. *Get it out of here.*

Tansy was still licking, her short tail quivering with delight. Old Scratch had to move her head aside before he could see what was what.

*Away my girl*, he crooned; *away awhile; be good.* And the old goat backed off, obediently enough, as he bent his aching knees and cautiously parted the straw.

His fingers, clumsy in their winter wrappings, touched and fumbled at the knobbles and bumps of what he still hoped would be a turnip. But vegetables, as he'd acknowledged already, don't yowl like little banshees. Nor would one have latched onto the tip of his longest finger and started to suck.

*By all the . . .*

A bite, or a sting, would have shocked him less. He snatched his fingers away, wiped the sucked one on his sleeve and then, in one quick movement, flung the straw aside.

A baby.

It was a baby lying there; newborn and bloodied; its face all slippy with goat drool, and stuff from its mother's womb. It had stopped its crying and Old Scratch thought it must have died, it lay so still—an effigy-of-a-child—staring up with eyes as black and blank as poke-holes in the snow.

Old Scratch tutted, then jabbed the baby in the twigs of its ribs. *Gone,* he thought, pragmatically. *As dead as a pebble.*

But the infant wasn't gone. And as Old Scratch hauled it up in both his rag-bound hands, solemnly noting its maleness, intending to bury it deep, somewhere so that foxes wouldn't get it, it jerked like a thing in a trap and began to struggle, and to scream, with such determined fury that Old Scratch almost dropped it.

Appalled, he held the slippery, screaming thing at arm's length. It hung from his fingers like a skinned rabbit—a flayed and gore-smeared creature that somehow, against enormous odds, still lived.

'Hush! Be quiet!'

If it had been a goat—an abandoned kid—he would have known exactly what to do: leave it with a surrogate and let nature take its course. Would a doe suckle a human child? It made him squeamish just to think of it. Certainly his Tansy could not be relied upon to nurture this small human. She had almost eaten its head.

Behind him, the goats were stamping and

bumping and crying out in rising alarm. Some of them needed milking.

*All right*, he soothed, in his calming voice. *It's all right, my goatlings, you have nothing to fear. It's all right . . .*

And he wedged the infant—purple-faced, now, and still howling—up in the place where fresh straw was stored, and got down to the business of milking.

His girls were skittish, flinching from his touch, and their milk came in anxious spurts. By the time he was done, the baby had, once again, fallen silent and he couldn't help but hope that, this time, it was for ever. Its chances of survival were so slight, after all, that better it died now than later. Less to suffer.

Only . . .

Sighing, Old Scratch returned to the spot where he had stashed the infant, and looked. The baby stared back at him, and mewled. *It—he—has a soul,* Old Scratch reminded himself. *A soul with nowhere to go, should it die here, with just me and my goats to mark its passing.*

And so he dabbled his fingers in the pail of fresh milk, and let the infant suck. Then he swaddled it as best he could, with the wrappings from his own hands, before tucking it under his arm, like a poacher's kill, and taking it outside.

*That man . . . that girl . . .* They would be long gone by now, Old Scratch supposed. Long gone, and giddy with relief. 'Blasts and fogs upon the both of ye,' he muttered, as he followed, slithering, the marks left by the sledge: marks already melting, as if warmed from underneath. 'May every hour—every minute—of your time left on this earth be heavy with remorse. May the weight of it give you crooked spines, may the mewling of small creatures forever break your sorry hearts, and the snows of winter chill you with the memory of Old Scratch and your ill-use of his charity and his premises.'

As he hobbled, still muttering, past his own shack, the baby twisted to look up at him. And the expression on its face was both satisfied and knowing, as if a lullaby of curses was sweet music to its ears.

# IV

'Annie? Are you awake my dear? Old Scratch has desperate need of you.'

'Desperate is it? Why so, by all the saints?'

'He'll explain, dear. I'm sending him up.'

'Samuel John Huckle! Has fatherhood addled your wits? This is women's space up here. My time for lying in. Old Scratch has no more business in this chamber than a jackdaw in a dovecote. Pray deal with him yourself.'

Sam Huckle cleared his throat.

'He has a babby with him,' he called up the ladder. 'A foundling, hours old.'

The gossips seated round Annie Huckle's bed looked sideways at one another, each wondering, with glinting eyes, whose infant this might be, and how come Old Scratch had a hold of it. Was he the father? Surely not. Two of them guffawed, tickled by the very idea.

Beside the bed, in a cradle made from a fallen tree, a day-old baby girl slumbered on, contented.

Old Scratch shuffled, unhappily, at the foot of the ladder and adjusted his grip on the foundling. He was holding it properly now, and getting used to its wriggles, and the way it stared so resignedly, with its poke-hole eyes, as if it had been in the world for a very long time and nothing, including death, would come to it as any great surprise.

'The monastery,' he said to Sam Huckle—loudly, so that the women would hear, and decisively, to discourage further teasing. 'I'll take him there. Would have gone to the monks in the first place but thought to myself: Annie does baptisms and will know of a wet-nurse too. Kill two birds with one stone, I thought. Didn't know, hadn't heard, that Annie herself was . . .'

'Is it stiff, Old Scratch?'

'Beg pardon?'

The gossips cackled. Sam Huckle shook his head. *Women.* 'They mean the infant, Scratch,' he said, kindly. 'They mean, is the infant in a state of *rigor mortis*, and beyond all human intervention. Pay them no mind.' Then: 'Annie,' he hollered, upwards. 'Have a heart, woman. Those old monks don't have a clue. They'd save this foundling's soul and then try and feed it turnips. They'd talk to it in Latin, then forget all about it during evensong—and right through until matins too, I shouldn't wonder. We're passing it up.'

He beckoned to Old Scratch, to give the baby to him, and Old Scratch was glad to do so. He didn't want to see those gossips, or Annie either; had no desire to enter a birthing chamber with its strange smells, and peculiar rituals, and all those women looking down their noses at him as if the very fact of his maleness might taint the air, or soil the linen, or cause the newly-delivered mother an extra twinge or two of pain.

The baby blinked its age-old eyes at him. *So you're off then, are you?* it seemed to be thinking. *Fine. All right. Begone then, just like my mother, and my father too, whoever he was . . .*

The ceiling was low and the ladder short. Sam Huckle reached up, a gossip reached down, saying, 'All right, give the little stinker here, if you must,' and the baby was gone.

'I'll have my wrappings back some time,' Old Scratch called out, moving backwards, away from the ladder. 'And . . .' He hesitated, surprised by an idea that had slipped into his head; 'And . . . the babby too, if it's spared . . . Not yet,' he added, almost tripping over the hearth in his hurry to be gone. 'Later. Once it's weaned. Grown bigger—taller—able to talk sense and climb a stile. Could do with a boy, I could, to help with my goats. Not getting any younger . . .'

And off he hobbled, out of the house and away, before either Sam or Annie Huckle could protest: about the cost, more than anything, of raising a foundling to boyhood, and about the bare-faced cheek of Old Scratch for imposing one on them, at a difficult time.

But they would do the right thing, Old Scratch felt sure, because they were good people. They would coddle that foundling as if he was their own, and get their reward in Heaven. *I'll leave milk outside their door on a regular basis,* he decided. *Meat too, now and then, if I can spare it. I'll do my bit, when I can; on days when the weather is fair and my bones don't ache and the goats don't need my full attention.*

All around him the snow was melting; turning lanes to streams and fields to bogs. He squinted up at the sun, risen now and surprisingly hot, and told himself that every child deserved a chance, and that a babby left in a goat shack, to die of starvation, or be eaten, like a root, deserved one more than most.

Passing the gates to the monastery he considered calling in. The infant's mother had spoken of a boy there, sending the sledge in the wrong direction. He'd guessed, she'd said. Guessed what? If it was the boy he knew—the one who sometimes brought him eggs—there would be no point questioning him on the matter, for he was as mute as a shadow on a wall. Never said boo to a goose. And anyway, the girl might have lied. Probably had lied, in fact, for what price honesty when you could discard your own infant, flesh of your flesh, like peel ripped from an orange?

*Bah!*

It came to Old Scratch, as he hurried on, that the girl might have had no intention of finding Annie Huckle. That for her son to have been born in the middle of nowhere, with no one to say she should

23

suckle him, or swaddle him, or even take him home, might have suited her very nicely.

*Fiendish girl,* he muttered, beginning to sweat from his hurrying, and from the unseasonable warmth of the sun. *You took the wrong road on purpose, didn't you? Bah! May your hair turn silver overnight . . . May the sight of a goat, or the taste of its cheese, make you puke like a swirled herring . . . May . . .*

Home now, he swiped up his jug and platter, from the stone outside his door. The snow was dripping so fast, from what passed for his roof, that his shack appeared to be weeping.

Something rattled, metal against tin. He tipped the jug upside down; saw the glint of something as it fell; missed catching it, and had to bend and go a-fumbling in a puddle of slush and mud. And out of the puddle he plucked a ring. A ring with a stone in it, the colour of dried blood.

*Hah!* he thought. *Recompense is it? A little something for Old Scratch's trouble? It will be made of fool's gold then, and that stone not worth a sneeze. For, as surely as I stand here, that feckless pair would never have left a thing of any value for one such as I.*

Only later did he discover the handkerchief, stuck fast to the inside of the jug. It was white, with a border of lace, and there were words daubed on it that were exactly the same colour as the stone in the ring.

Old Scratch, who could not read and had never held a pen, saw only that each letter was smudged and badly formed. He assumed that this was just how writing looked when it had been done, in haste, on a handkerchief, and left outdoors in a jug. He didn't guess, and never would, that they had been picked out, laboriously, with a wisp of straw dipped and dabbed in birth-blood.

The other assumption Old Scratch made was that this message had been penned by the man. A gentleman, he vaguely supposed, would carry quill and ink on him at all times, just in case he was called upon to make his mark—to prove himself as a person of high standing in this world. He imagined that the words on the handkerchief said, 'Sorry for ill-using you' or, 'Here's her ring. Keep it.' Something placatory, anyway, and of little consequence now that the couple had fled, with no intention, he was certain, of ever coming back.

The ring went into a hollow log, placed well away from Old Scratch's miserly fire and from the other logs, on barricade duty. Old Scratch kept his knife and spoon in there, a rosary made from acorns, and any bits of money he made from the sale of goats' milk, skins and cheese,

Remembering the three silver coins, hidden in his clothes, he took them out, wrapped them in the girl's handkerchief and stuffed the little bundle in beside the ring.

If the foundling was spared, he decided, he would give him his mother's ring when he was full-grown.

Worthless though it surely was, it was still the boy's, by rights, so let him have it. And one of the monks would be able to say what was written on the handkerchief. One day, should he or the boy decide—be bothered enough—to ask.

If it Lives
Beware it

# V

Annie Huckle called the foundling Jack. His screams, as she baptized him, were enough to worry the dead. The holy water she splashed on his forehead made him writhe, as if in pain, and when she traced the sign of the holy cross on him he went rigid, and was sick.

'Well, you little crosspatch . . .' Mopping him clean, Annie laughed to see so much outrage on such a tiny face. 'That's your soul saved, so you be a good boy now and may God grant you life, or take you speedily to his bliss.'

One of the gossips clucked and sighed. 'It comes to something Annie, don't it,' she said, 'knowing that some common chit left this healthy boy to die while the King of England prays daily for a son, and the Spanish Queen, God grant her strength, delivers him only stillborns, and a girl.'

'It does indeed,' said Annie. 'Let us offer up a prayer, my ladies, for King Henry and Queen Catherine.'

'For Queen Catherine alone, I'd say,' another gossip remarked. 'For she needs all the prayers she can get, poor lady, now that she is of a certain age and that temptress, Anne Boleyn, be playing fast and loose with the King.'

Annie winced. 'Kate Bundy,' she scolded. 'You talk like you've come fresh from court to bide a while with us country folk. How can you know such things?'

Her friend raised her eyebrows. 'Words travel,' she said. 'If you came to the market like the rest of us, Annie, you'd hear all kinds.'

'Hmm.' The prayer forgotten, Annie gave Jack's watchful face another dab.

'Will you keep him, Annie?' a gossip asked. 'If he's spared? Will you raise him for a goatherd, like Old Scratch wants, or give him to the monks?'

Annie shrugged against her pillows. 'I'll keep him,' she said. 'For now.' And she swaddled Jack in fresh linen, and passed him to the nearest gossip, who set him down in the cradle, beside the Huckles' newborn girl.

'A thorn beside a rose,' the gossip said. 'They couldn't be more different, Annie, could they?' The baby girl, aware of change, woke up. Beside her, Jack blinked. Head to head they were, but too tightly swaddled to move.

Annie Huckle, more exhausted than she had expected to be, after feeding such a mite of a newborn boy-child, leant from the bed to peer into the cradle. Two pairs of eyes, heaven blue and raven black, met hers.

'There now,' she crooned, reaching down to stroke her daughter's cheek. 'There now, Janet. You have a little friend.'

# VI

Jack was spared. It would be said, in years to come, that the Devil looks after his own. But in those first weeks of his life it was Annie Huckle who did all the looking after, determined that any foundling left in her brisk yet tender care should not only live but thrive. And, oh, how that boy thrived. He grew so big and strong that by the time he and Janet Huckle were two moons old he was taking up most of the cradle. 'Like a cuckoo,' Annie chuckled, tickling him under his chins. 'A cuckoo in the nest.' She was fond of Jack back then. He was just a babby, after all, albeit a greedy one with strangely knowing eyes.

Sam Huckle made a second, larger, cradle and slid Jack into it. Jack howled. So did Janet. And they carried on howling, inconsolable, until they were placed together again, side by side, head to head, in the longer, wider space.

Out of swaddling, and into gowns, they slept face to face, breathing, damply, into each other's mouths and noses. When one woke, so did the other. When Janet cried, flame-cheeked from cutting a tooth, Jack shrieked in sympathy. They learned to walk early, holding hands and tottering, gamely, across the Huckles' back lawn. Birds in the trees called out, in alarm, but Annie Huckle smiled. *Just look at them*, she thought. *My little girl and the foundling boy. How dear they are together, he so dark and she so fair. How quaint.'*

'Jack!' Annie or Sam would call out, and both Jack and Janet would turn their heads. 'Janet!' the same. It was as if both children only heard, or paid attention to, that first syllable: "Ja". Had they been able to speak they might have explained, together, and in unison, that it actually didn't matter whose name was being called. They felt like one person and always would.

JanetandJack.

JackandJanet.

By the time they were two they had their own language: an incoherent babble full of rasps and guttural noises which, at times, sounded feral, as if two wolf cubs were at play. As days and weeks passed, the babble grew more sophisticated, with accents, and stresses and sudden yelps of mirth.

Wild though she sometimes sounded, Janet was a dainty child, neat-limbed and light on her toes. She loved to dance—preferred it to walking, it seemed, as she rarely moved anywhere, after finding her feet, without hopping, or skipping, or sliding across a floor with studied precision. Once in a while she would take herself into the garden, or the middle of the downstairs room, to perform something of her own devising: part waltz, part baby-stagger. And the

Huckles would applaud, thinking *sweetness*, while Jack sat very still and watched.

Although nimble enough himself, Jack never tried to dance. Nor did he ever clap, or smile, when Janet did, although, once, Annie thought she heard him humming, low in his throat, as if trying to match a tune to Janet's movements.

'Go on Jack,' she'd said on that occasion, 'dance, then.' But he hadn't. *He's bashful*, she'd assumed. *Worried about being looked upon.* But after a while it dawned on Annie: Jack wasn't bashful. Shyness didn't come into it. He simply didn't *want* to dance, and watching Janet do it, contented and alone, vexed him. It took her away.

*A sulker*, she thought, then. *That's what this boy's turning into. A proper wet lettuce.* But it began to be more than that.

When the children were three, Jack began to experience what Annie called his 'glooms'. At odd times, and without any warning, he would scoot under the family's table and remain there, scowling out, and blinking, very fast, as if his eyelids were suddenly sore.

The first few times this happened Annie tried coaxing him out, and back to rights, with rhymes and banter and scraps of sugar dough. But only Janet could soothe him. Only Janet, by stroking Jack's hands, and crooning to him in that peculiar language they shared, could lift whatever darkness had surrounded, or entered, the boy.

Those glooms gave Annie the shivers. 'He'll grow out of them,' Sam said. 'Have patience, wife, and leave him be. For what harm does he do, after all?'

*None,* Annie thought, *that you or I can see, Sam Huckle. But, then, harm has many guises. It can swirl in the air, harm can, as silent as dust, and get to you as surely as any kick or fisty-blow such as a normal child would aim, while in a nasty mood.*

'As you will, husband,' she said, knowing there to be no point in voicing her fears to a man who—God love him—saw only good in those whose true colours had yet to surface. 'As you will, Sam Huckle. I just pray that you are right.'

It was some three weeks after this that little Janet was given The Present: a young singing bird, in a willow-wood cage. It came from a woman delivered, by Annie, of a healthy baby girl—a longed-for daughter, and a sister for six little boys.

'My girl . . . my girl . . .' the new mother had cried, unable to believe her luck. 'You have a girl, Annie, don't you? Well, I would give to her a present. No . . . no . . . I insist. Unhook you that bird cage from the beam over there and take it with you when you go. For I feel so blessed, Annie Huckle, that I must do a kind deed, quick sharp, lest the saints deem me unworthy and take this bliss away.'

Janet was delighted with her gift. So much so that she uttered what Annie took to be her first coherent word.

'Out,' she said and her fingers moved over the cage, seeking a way to open it. The bird stepped sideways along its perch, to get as close to her face as possible, and the cheeps and chirrups it directed at her were like kisses being blown. Pausing, Janet chuckled into the cage and aimed two kisses of her own at the bird's tiny beak. 'Out,' she said again, turning, expectantly, to Jack. 'Out, Ja. Out.'

As quick as a wink Annie stepped forward. 'Not out,' she insisted, lifting the cage high above her head, before Jack could get his hands on it. 'The little bird is all right where he is, Jannie. Come, we'll hang his house in the window space. He'll be happy there.'

Jack stayed back, frowning, while Annie and her daughter saw to the cage. 'This is Janet's bird,' Annie said to him. 'Not yours, Jack. Janet's. Do you understand?'

It seemed Jack did, for he made no attempt to approach the cage, once it was in the window, and, after a while, as Annie and Janet continued to coo up at the little bird, he turned away as if this new addition to the family held no interest for him at all.

After supper, Sam Huckle swung Janet onto his shoulders so that she could feed the bird its peck of corn. 'Out?' she asked, again, but her father, too, said no, so she blew the bird more kisses, pressing her mouth right up against the struts of the cage. The bird twittered happily, its beak almost touching her lower lip.

'He loves you, Jannie!' Annie said. 'He loves you to distraction.'

At his place beside the hearth, Jack blinked and clenched his fists.

# VII

It was Sam who, rising early the next day, found the bird cage under the table, up-ended. Two of its struts had been snapped, like ribs, to make a space easily big enough for a small hand to reach in, or a small bird to fly out. The back door stood open. It had been closed the night before, and bolted, Sam could vouch for that.

'Annie,' Sam called up the ladder. 'Come down and look at this.'

Annie ranted. Annie raved. Only the nastiest of boys, she insisted, would have conceived of such a trick. Their Jannie would be heartbroken—inconsolable. What was Sam going to do about it? And how, in the Devil's name, had that wretched foundling crept down, in the dead of night, without waking the rest of them up? And furthermore . . .

'Annie . . .' Tom placed a steadying hand on his wife's arm and nodded towards the foot of the ladder. Whirling round, Annie found Jack, and Janet standing there, shoulder to shoulder, in their identical nightgowns. Jack was yawning; rubbing his eyes. Janet was gazing, sadly, at the broken cage.

Annie felt her heart contract. 'Come here, Jannie,' she said, holding out her arms.

But Janet didn't move. 'Out' she said, her voice bleak as she reached for Jack's hand.

'Jack,' said Sam. 'Did you do this?' He pointed to the cage. Jack considered the thing and then nodded. 'Out,' he said, and the word, coming from him, sounded proud, but with just enough of a tremor to suggest uncertainty. *I thought I'd done the right thing,* said that 'out'. *But you're angry with me aren't you, Sam Huckle? So now I'm a little confused.*

Beside him, Janet sniffed.

Sam looked at Annie—*what am I to do?*—then across at his little girl.

'Did you know about this, Jannie?' he asked, gently. 'Did you want the little bird set loose? Is that it?'

Janet Huckle sighed. One tear ... two ... rolled down her face and she gave the tiniest sob. Jack dropped her hand. Then, with an almighty wail, he raised one arm to his eyes and pressed it there, as if staunching an almighty wave of sorrow with his sleeve.

*Why, you cunning little* ... Two steps towards him, Annie took, before Sam grabbed the strings of her gown and held her back.

'Return to your bed,' Sam told the children. 'It is too early for you to be up. Go back to sleep, if you can, my dears, and ... and worry no more about the bird. It will have found itself a pretty tree, by now, and others of its kind.'

36

'They thought they were setting it free,' he whispered to his wife as first Janet, then Jack, went scampering up the ladder.

Annie jerked herself away from him, and sat, heavily, on a bench. She felt like a sack, emptied out. She felt, suddenly, very old.

'I don't think they meant any harm,' Sam persisted. 'They just didn't think it through.'

'Hah!' Annie tried to picture the bird; pecked to death by a crow, or dissolving in a fox's stomach. 'Our Jannie would have meant well.' she said. 'But he . . . he just wanted it gone.'

'Oh, Annie . . .' Sam scratched at his chin, perplexed. 'He wouldn't do that, would he? Not to Jannie. He dotes on her.' He picked up the cage. 'Kindling for the fire?' he asked. 'Or shall we mend it, and then wait a day or two, in case the bird comes back?'

He sounded, and looked, so hopeful that Annie had to smile. And later, while pegging out the washing, she caught herself listening out for the little bird's song. After all, she told herself, she had no proof, yet, that it was dead. And if Sam could hope for the best, well . . . so, perhaps, could she.

Would the little bird have remembered how to fly? she wondered, setting down her basket of pegs. Possibly not. So there was a chance, then, that it might have taken shelter somewhere; under a beehive, perhaps, or in among the plants.

37

She went to where her herbs were coming up in thick, sweet, clumps. Kneeling clumsily down on the path, she bent over the soil and began parting leaves and stalks. The good, clean, scents of rosemary and thyme sharpened her resolve. *If it's here, I'll find it*, she thought. *And if I do, and he troubles it again, there will be Hell to pay.*

Halfway along the path she had gone; inching sideways on her knees, when she spotted it. *Oh*, she breathed, reaching down then rearing away . . . not wanting to touch . . . unable to believe . . .

'Sam!' she cried out. 'Sam come quick!'

Thinking her injured, Sam ran. 'Stay in,' he ordered the children as they followed, hand in hand, 'Don't come out.' He could see Annie through the doorway, down on her knees, both hands pressed to her mouth.

'Whatever is it?' he panicked. 'Are you hurt? Was it a bee?'

And then he was beside her, down on his own knees the better to see what ailed her. 'Whatever is it?' he repeated. 'What?'

She didn't answer, only took one hand away from her mouth, and pointed.

Looking down, Sam saw a stone.

'Oh,' he said, all puzzlement. 'Did that hit you, dear? Did someone throw it over the wall? I don't . . .'

'Look at it.' Annie's voice was hushed. Appalled. Sam had never heard her speak that way before.

Confused, he looked back at the stone. He looked for a long time. Then: 'I don't understand,' he said, 'quite what it is I'm supposed to be seeing.'

Annie clutched at his arm. He felt her nails digging in. '*But surely,*' she hissed in his ear. '*Surely to God, Sam, you can see it as clear as a nose on a face. It's the bird! It's Jannie's bird!*'

Sam swallowed. Then he frowned. Then he bent very close to the stone as if he might be about to kiss it. It was the same *size* as the little bird, he granted Annie that. And the same colour, too, more or less. And, yes, all right, there was ridge—a raised curve—that could be said to resemble a wing. If you wanted it to. If you were not, for whatever reason, thinking straight and true.

He picked the stone up. Annie squawked and jumped to her feet.

The stone felt warm in the palm of Sam's hand. Warm, like a living creature. But then . . . the sun had been on it a while, had it not? He turned the thing over; felt its weight, and smiled a rueful smile.

'Annie,' he said. 'It's just a stone.'

Behind him, Annie tutted and huffed. 'I *know* it's a stone,' she said. 'But how did it become so is what I want to know. How did a living, breathing creature get to be this way? What wickedness—what *sorcery*—transformed it?'

'Oh, Annie . . .'

Sam dropped the stone on the path, stood up, and took his wife in his arms. She was over-wrought, he told himself. In need, perhaps, of a tonic. It crossed his mind that she might be with child again, for women, he knew, suffered all kinds of fancies at such a testing time.

'Are you . . .' he whispered into Annie's hair. 'Might you be . . . ?'

She smacked at his arm. 'Samuel John Huckle,' she scolded. 'Of all the daft things to say!'

Sam held her a moment longer. Over her shoulder he noticed the children. They were standing in the doorway; staying in, as he'd instructed. Janet had her thumb in her mouth and her head against Jack's shoulder. Neither she nor Jack looked worried; only puzzled and rather bored. Still, Sam thought, you never could tell, with children. 'It's all right,' he mouthed at them, behind his wife's back. 'Everything is well.'

Later, without having to be told, Sam took the stone from the garden and walked with it to the lake. He felt foolish doing this but *needs must*, he thought, as he strode, purposefully, along the lane, the stone held tight in his fist.

He passed a boy coming away from the lake with bundles of reeds on his back. The boy's hands were bleeding from umpteen shallow cuts and Sam wondered at the stupidity of harvesting reeds, without protection, until he recognized the boy as the lad from the monastery. The lad who sang, but never spoke. Such a lad, Sam knew, would suffer the mortification of a thousand cuts rather than wear gloves to work the reed beds. The greater the pain, the greater the penance. The boy's fingers were swollen, as well as lacerated, yet his face, as he nodded to Sam a silent greeting, was radiant. Beatific.

'Go well,' Sam responded, ashamed, suddenly, of his own ridiculous errand and unaccountably afraid lest this boy should divine, somehow, that his beloved Annie had believed an ordinary stone bewitched. Holy men, he reminded himself, had strict views about such things. So it would bode very ill indeed for Annie—for the whole family—should any monk hereabouts learn of her strange fancies and reckon them the Devil's work.

He considered turning back, then. Imagined himself putting the stone back where Annie had found it and saying sternly, to her face: 'I won't pander to your nonsense, wife. It's a common garden pebble. Live with it.' Yet Annie, being Annie, would let the bees swarm, the gooseberries rot and the herbs fall all to seed rather than set foot in the garden, knowing the stone to be there, still. Best to nip things in the bud, Sam told himself, and let life return to normal.

Alone, beside the lake, he examined the stone again. Just to be sure. Just to be absolutely certain that his wife's strange fancy had no rhyme to it, or reason. Three times he turned the stone over, waiting . . . wondering . . . daring it to sprout feathers, and to fly, singing, from his hand into the cold March sky. Then: *What nonsense,* he berated himself. *What moonshine.* His throw was a good one, fast and true. *That's that, then,* he thought turning away, satisfied, as his daughter's fossilized singing bird hit the lake, and sank.

# VIII

Annie never mentioned the stone again. She told herself that Sam had been right about it. That she had formed a ridiculous fancy, based on its colour, and size, and a flaw that resembled a wing.

Of one thing, though, she remained absolutely certain: little Janet was going to have to start thinking, speaking and acting for herself. Her bond with the foundling had grown too tight—too *adult*, somehow. It would have to be loosened, like swaddling. And soon.

She waited until Sam went out, one day, to chop and gather wood. Then: 'flower,' she said to Janet, pointing to a cowslip. And then, 'blue sky', 'ribbon' and 'spoon'. 'Wall,' she said to Jack, and 'feet', and 'holly bush', and 'shadow'.

It was late spring; the Huckles' back garden full of buds and fledglings and pale, clear light. Annie, perched on the edge of a stone bench, had been spooning curds and whey into the children's mouths as they stood, hand in hand, in front of her. '*One for Janet, one for Jack, the old brown cart goes clacketty clack . . .*'

Both children had eaten quickly—obediently—but had either of them, Annie wondered, paid attention to the rhyme? Had they found pleasure and comfort in the ritual of her saying it, like any normal boy and girl? She knew that they had not. They were too absorbed, one with the other, to care what she, or anyone else, had to say, or sing, around them.

When the dish was clean, Annie set it down on the bench, then grabbed each child by a sleeve, before either could run away. She would have them talking the King's English by suppertime, she promised herself; even if it was only a couple of words apiece.

Their babbling—that secret code they shared—was no longer quaint. It was unnatural.

'Sky,' she repeated to Janet, scooping the child onto her lap and holding her there when she wriggled to get down. 'Feet,' she said, sternly, to Jack, keeping him at arm's length; tightening her grip on him as he scrabbled and pushed, wanting to be up on her knees, with Janet.

'Say "feet" Jack. Go on.'

But Jack did not say feet. Instead, he broke free and went charging across the lawn, his dark head lowered, as if he might butt a tree; his own feet skidding on worms and dew.

Janet remained, politely, on her mother's lap, but her eyes followed Jack as he rampaged around the garden—not hurting anything; not kicking a beehive, or beheading the cowslips; just blundering, angrily, looking up every few seconds to catch Janet's glance. To be sure of her attention.

'Sky,' Annie said, surprised by the tremor in her voice; by how very important it had become for her to win this battle of wills. 'Blue sky, Janet. You can say it, sweetling. Sky . . . sky . . . *sky*.' She said the word over and over, until it felt odd in her mouth: a sliver of a word, sucked of all meaning.

'Ska,' Janet said, eventually, taking her eyes off Jack to point upwards. 'Blue ska.'

'Good girl!' Annie held her daughter close, nuzzling the floss of her hair. 'My angel . . . my all.' Suddenly, there was Jack, standing right in front of her; tugging, with both hands, at the hem of Janet's smock.

'Mine,' he insisted, twisting his fingers in the cloth. 'My Ja.'

Annie swallowed hard. Jack's voice, she noticed, was more like a man's than a small boy's, and a rough-and-ready man's, at that. It had, she supposed, always been on the gruff side, but while he'd only been a-babbling, lying flat on his back in the cradle, or plonked on his bottom somewhere, talking his own talk, the menace of it had escaped her.

'Let go, Jack,' she scolded, aware that she sounded scared, and that her heart was thumping nineteen to the dozen although it was nonsense . . . *nonsense* . . . that she, a grown woman, should feel threatened so, by a child barely out of clouts and no bigger than an elf. 'Let go of her, you bad boy.' But Jack would not let go. And Janet, far from minding, leaned towards him, beaming.

'My Ja,' she echoed, her small hands fluttering as she reached to pat his face. 'Mine.'

Abruptly, Annie stood, yanking her daughter up with her. As she rose, she knocked the pudding dish. The sound of it striking the path and breaking made her wince. *I was fond of that dish*, she thought. *I will mind about it, later, when I have dealt with this . . . this . . .*

The sudden strain on her, as she straightened up, took her so much by surprise that had it been a cat, or a marrow, or even somebody else's child in the crook of her left arm. she would have dropped it. Instinctively, and in the nick of time, she tightened her grip, and braced herself against the edge of the bench, managing—just—to keep her balance, and her hold on her child.

It was *Jack* . . . Jack, she saw, had risen with her, clinging fast to Janet's smock. His bare feet were paddling the air . . . bashing her shins . . . his knuckles turning white from the strain of hanging on.

Appalled, Annie leaned even further backwards to counterbalance the pull, to stop the boy's weight from strangling Janet with the collar of her smock, or from bringing the poor little mite down onto the path, where her head would surely crack and break, just like the pudding dish.

'Let go!' she shrieked, lashing out with her free hand 'Let go—*get away*! You're too heavy . . .'

Jack's face, staring up, was shocking. *I have her, Mother Huckle*, said the leer on it. *And there is nothing you can do about it.*

Annie lashed out harder—hard enough, she knew, to raise bruises and welts. *May the saints forgive me*, she thought, landing wallops where she could . . . feeling the raw sting on her own palm as she caught Jack's left arm, his shoulder, the side of his head, his cheek. *This is wrong, what I'm doing . . . striking such a little boy so . . . but he mustn't win . . . I dare not let him win.*

When a flurry of kicks caught her in the kidneys she almost lost her grip; almost dropped both children, hard, onto the ground. 'Why, you little . . .' she blurted downwards. And then she realized: it wasn't Jack, contorting his legs somehow, to hammer at her belly with his heels, it was *Janet*, little Janet, fighting her own mother with calculated fury; as hell bent on getting to Jack as he was on getting to her.

Those kicks . . . they reminded Annie, with a bitter-sweet pang, of the way her girl had kicked in the womb: lightly, without malice, not so very long ago. *I cannot have this. I cannot . . .*

'Jack,' she heard herself say, 'You are hurting your Ja. If you don't let go *right now* you will maim her.'

*He won't understand*, she thought, a sob catching in her throat. *I'm wasting my breath here.* And even as she thought it, her breath caught, like the sob. Not wasted, but trapped. Stuck in her gullet like a fistful of nuts, or an apple swallowed whole. And the length of her throat . . . and the whole of her chest . . . felt so *heavy*, suddenly, it was as if . . . as if . . .

She thought of the bird. Of the stone with the ridge like a folded wing. She thought of statues, and then of gargoyles as her face twisted in a silent scream.

Then Jack let go. So suddenly that he fell flat on his spine, and knocked his head on the path. Annie gasped as her throat cleared and her lungs filled and the terrible heaviness left her chest, like armour being removed.

*Thank God*, she thought. *Thank God*... Janet had stopped kicking, and was frantic to get down. Trembling; using both arms now to hang on to her wriggling daughter—*How did I not drop her? How?* —Annie watched Jack sit up.

'Ouch!' he said, rubbing his crown. And the face that he pulled was the kind of face any little boy might pull when he knows he is in trouble: rueful, appealing and just a little bit afraid.

'Get up,' Annie ordered him. *Keep everything normal*, she told herself. *Your voice. The morning. Everything.* 'We will go indoors now,' she said as calmly as she could. 'Are you listening, Jack? Good. We will go indoors and make broth; a good broth with nutmeg and barley and peas. You and Janet will mix dough for dumplings with the big wooden spoon. Then I will tell you the story about Nelly and Ned, lost in a forest, with only a trail of breadcrumbs to lead them back home, and that trail being eaten by robins...'

*Put little Janet down—that's right. And do not wince, or seem at all upset, when she runs to him—there she goes—or when he clings to her—yes—like a man in miniature, reclaiming a lost love. Stay very calm, Annie Huckle, until this day is over; until both of these children are sound asleep in their bed. Then do what must be done—what should have been done long before now. Get rid of him.*

# IX

Normally, Jack would have woken the instant he was touched. Lifting him away from his Ja, however late the hour, would have had him fully conscious in a heartbeat, roaring his displeasure to the rafters.

Normally.

'What have you done to him, woman?' Sam Huckle whispered, startled by the way Jack flopped against his shoulder, as limp as a stillborn pup. 'And to our Janet? She lies so pale and still. What are you . . .'

'Whissht,' Annie hissed through her teeth. 'Save your breath to cool your porridge, Sam Huckle. 'Tis only a sleeping draught, carefully measured. Do you think I would dose a child—any child—the same as a horse, or a person full grown? Have some faith, man, in all that I know and can do.'

Sam placed one hand against the sleeping boy's head. He had been told only so much about the incident in the garden. Jack's wilful disobedience. A smashed bowl. Annie's sudden turn—the heaviness in her chest—which had surely been her heart's response to too much agitation, and must never happen again.

'Are you sure about this, dear?' he said, over Jack's head. 'Is there really no other way?'

Annie eyed Jack's shape, moth-pale in its nightgown against the cloth of her husband's shirt. Despite the walloping she had given the boy there wasn't a mark on him. No bruises, no welts, no trace of a handprint on his cheek. It reminded her of how resilient Jack had always been to knocks and scrapes of any kind. Of how even a nasty tumble down the ladder, before he could walk, had left him undaunted and miraculously unhurt. And although he could holler fit to burst he had never, so far as Annie could remember, ever shed a single tear. It made her shudder, now, to think of it.

'As God is my witness,' she said to her husband. 'I want that foundling gone.'

The potion she had fed to Jack in a big spoonful of jam, should, she knew, have knocked him senseless until daybreak. He shouldn't even dream. And when he woke his memory would be a slippy, unreliable thing—wiped as clean as a slate, with any luck.

Annie trusted her potions. And yet . . . had Jack's eyes snapped open, as he lolled against her husband's shoulder, and his mouth curled in a snarl, she would not have been at all surprised.

'He has a dark heart,' she said. 'This boy . . . this foundling . . . has a heart as dark as sin. So take him, Sam, as far from here as you can ride and still be home by daybreak. Pick a clearing or a grassy knoll and leave him there. The nights are warmer, now, and

51

he is as fit as a butcher's cat. He will not perish from lying out under the stars awhile. Let others take pity on him, as they surely will, and raise him from now on. Only get him away from our daughter, and out of my sight. For good.'

Sam did as he was told—but not exactly. He took Jack away—but not as far as he could ride. He picked a place—but not any old place.

And he did not leave Jack under the stars or on a grassy knoll but kept the boy against his shoulder, for a final minute more, as he hammered on what passed for a door.

'Is that you, young Frizzle Face, disturbing an old man's rest? Trust a monkery boy to come a-knocking and a-banging whenever it suits ... God's breath!'

Old Scratch was astonished, and far from pleased, to find Sam Huckle on his threshold, and with a child—*the* child, he realized—with him. Told that the foundling was now his responsibility, he took two steps backwards, stumbled against a log and cursed some more.

'Can he talk sense yet?' he demanded, kicking the log aside. 'Can he climb a stile? I'm guessing not. Take him away, Sam Huckle. I would more easily walk to London town with bees in my beard and a mad dog at my heels than be with a boy of this age and size for any length of time. Come back in four—no, five— years. Good night to you. Regards to Annie.'

'Wait!'

Sam Huckle put one foot across the threshold. Old Scratch, looking down at it, remembered another foot, just as insistent: a foot in a boot of finest leather, invading his space; preventing him from putting back his door.

*If I was a younger man*, he thought, crossly, *and Sam Huckle anything less than a decent cove, I would kick that foot clear or drop a log on it. My biggest, heaviest log.*

Against Sam Huckle's shoulder, young Jack began to whimper, not surfacing yet but aware, on some level, that he had been parted from his Ja and that waking would bring more sorrow than he would know how to bear.

'It has to be now, Scratch,' Sam said. 'Annie can't cope. Not with two the same age. He's a strong lad, and a healthy one, and will be company for you, by and by, and a big help with the goats. His name is Jack, did you know?'

Old Scratch shook his head, just a little bit ashamed. He had meant, he truly had, to take milk to the Huckles, and meat too, and to show occasional interest in how the foundling fared. But he had done none of those things. The Huckles lived far enough away for him to have conveniently forgotten about the milk-and-meat pledge, and to have shelved the idea of the foundling, as a helper and companion, until the time came when he might want to consider it again.

'You've caught me all wrong-footed on the matter,' he protested, raising his hands in a *No* as Sam lifted Jack and made as if to hand him over, like a sack of onions, only thrumming with needs. 'I've no pallet for the boy. No food to spare. He'll wake up and be a-feared. He'll howl for Annie, and for you, and then what will Old Scratch do?'

'You'll manage,' Sam answered, looking all around the shack for somewhere to set Jack down. 'I'm sorry, Scratch, but there it is. Annie wants him gone. You wanted him back—at least that's the impression you left us with—so I've done what I thought would work best all round. I can't take him home and he's not to come a-visiting; not next week, next month, or ever. I mean it, Scratch. It would only unsettle him, and Annie too, and Janet, our little girl. It would only cause ructions and tearful scenes.'

*Ructions and tearful scenes* . . . Old Scratch wanted no part in those, not next week, next month or ever.

'All right,' he agreed. 'Put him down by the logs. If he's more trouble than he's worth, I'll give him to the monks.'

# X

JackandJanet.

JanetandJack.

Janet wept. Finding Jack gone, she wept as if her heart was cracking then ran, dizzily, all around the house and out into the garden, searching... searching...

'*Ja... my Ja... where?*'

She wouldn't eat. She couldn't rest. She didn't even dance. Round and round and up and down she wandered, keening like a widow, while her mother hovered in her wake, not knowing what to do.

'Is it done?' was all Annie Huckle had asked when she woke with a start at dawn, to find Sam in the bed beside her, sleepless and out of sorts.

'It is,' was all he had replied, his tone so disapproving of the whole sorry business that Annie had swallowed her second question ('Where did you leave him, then?') and resolved to keep it down. It was enough, she told herself, as she drifted back to sleep, that Jack was gone. Best not to harp on about it. Best to let it lie.

At that first day's end, Janet stood at the garden gate, looking out across the lane. Beyond the lane were woods stretching, so far as Janet knew, to the edge of the known world. *My . . .* she murmured, sadly. resting her forehead against the gate. *My Ja . . .* The gate was locked, and would remain so until the autumn; until Annie Huckle was as sure as she would ever be that her daughter no longer pined for her cradle-friend, and would not go trying to find him.

Sam Huckle gave Janet a kitten, to keep in the house as a pet. The kitten was female and six shades of grey. Annie made a baby out of a clothes peg—a fist-sized little poppet which she dressed in a sprigged cotton gown and slid into her daughter's hand one night, to be there, as if by magic, when the little girl opened her eyes.

Janet ignored both the kitten and the toy. 'Pretty kitty,' her mother pleaded. And 'blue sky' and 'roses' and 'jam'. But Janet turned her head away, deaf to all words, even lovely ones, and as stubborn, in her grief, as a swan. She ate when she was told to eat, slept when put to bed, and got up at the appropriate hour, holding her arms up, at the correct angle, to be dressed for the day ahead.

Then, one boiling afternoon in mid-July, with Sam and Annie Huckle at their wits' end, the kitten—grown bigger now and aggravated, perhaps, by the heat, or neglect, or both—showed its nasty side by scratching Janet's face.

'Oh!' Janet cried out. 'Bad Ja. Naughty. Why?' And as the young cat streaked away, to hide under a beehive, she followed it, then coaxed it out, then sat it on her lap and stroked it over and over, until it purred with delight, befriended, at last, and forgiven.

'Pretty kitty,' Janet told it. 'Good kitty now. Mine.'

That night she slept with the cat at her feet and the peg baby clutched tight in one hand. The following morning she hugged her mother, kissed her father's cheek, and pirouetted round the garden. After that she grew as sweetly and as normally as any other little girl blessed with loving parents, enough to eat, and a placid disposition. In short, she began to get over the loss of her Ja and to find her own pleasures in the hours and days, then weeks and months, without him.

For Annie Huckle it was as if the sun had come out after a long and challenging winter. She gave thanks for the change in her daughter. She assumed all would be well.

Jack, meanwhile, felt the pain of separation like the loss of a limb: something permanent, from which he would never recover. Finding himself in a strange and not-very-comfortable place worked like salt in the wound.

Waking, that first morning, he blinked, howled, and attacked the barricade of logs with such strength, for one so little, that Old Scratch was impressed.

*Gipsy blood will out*, Scratch thought. *He's his mother's brat all right.* 'You need to calm down,' he told the boy. 'This is your home now, here with me and my goats. The other is far away. Forget it. I don't want to have to tie you up, but I will if you aren't good. I saved your life, you little whelp. That and your soul. Don't make me wish I hadn't.'

Jack snarled. He picked up a log and hurled it, missing what passed for Old Scratch's dinner plate by a whisker. Then he threw himself, face down, on the dirt floor and stayed there, trembling. He stayed there for so long that Old Scratch began to wonder if he was defective in some way: a liability palmed off by those Huckles with not one word of advice on how an old man might manage an imbecile who raged one minute, lay mute the next, and would be as much use around the goats as a box of fireworks.

'Eat,' he coaxed, pushing pellets of coarse bread against Jack's unhappy mouth. 'Or die. Up to you . . .'

*Die*, Jack thought, dully, turning his head away. *What is die?*

He ought to have found out. Any other three-year-old would have done, after refusing all sustenance for the best part of a week. Old Scratch, having really no idea how long a small child might survive without food or drink, could only watch, frustrated, and try different temptations and tricks: the last of his eggs, boiled and mashed . . . goats' milk sloshed, without warning, against the boy's cracked lips . . . a sliver of cheese posted onto his tongue, while he slept.

Even in sleep, sensing supper in his mouth, Jack spat and snarled and bit the hand that fed him. No goat had ever caused so much trouble. Old Scratch wedged straw beneath Jack's body and changed it, grumbling. when it became wet or soiled. At night he fetched sacks to keep Jack warm and sat up late, keeping a cross yet anxious vigil. 'Lullay,' he rasped in a poor attempt at song. 'Lullay lu. Sleep, now, do. While angels watch and . . . something, something . . . Lu la lu.'

Every day, coming back from tending his goats, Scratch pondered the odds on finding the child dead, vanished, or sitting up. To begin with, either of the first two scenarios would have suited him well enough. He would have shrugged, thought *so be it*, and got on with the rest of his life. By the seventh day, however, he had begun to feel something; some vague attachment . . . some measure of responsibility . . . towards the cussed little mite who lay in the shack, like one of the logs, only fading . . . surely fading, with every hour that passed.

*I must get him to the monastery,* Old Scratch thought then. *Let the monks tend to him. I must carry him a second time, to save his sorry life. And what thanks will I get for it? None, except in Heaven, which seems as remote, sometimes, and as difficult to get into, as any fortress here on earth.*

Young Jack would have loathed the monastery. All that chanting would have damaged his ears. The smell of incense would have turned his stomach and he would have kicked the shins of any monk who tried to make him learn a psalm.

The monks would have been concerned, at first, then alarmed, and finally suspicious. They might have tested Jack, one day ... might have made him touch their splinter from the Holy Cross, or plunged his arms, up to the points of his elbows, into a pail of holy water.

And the conclusion the monks would have come to, as they watched Jack writhe, would have been the same one Annie Huckle had reached before sending him away: that this boy was bad to the bone, and dangerous to know.

And then what?

*What might the monks have done then?*

But, again, young Jack was spared. For on the very day Old Scratch decided to give him to the monks, the boy known as Frizzle Face came to the shack, bringing fresh eggs, and such a palpable air of religious devotion that Jack had to move to escape it.

They met on the path, Old Scratch and the boy, and entered the shack together. Straightaway, Jack lifted his head, sniffing the air as if a gust of something noxious had blown in. Then he got himself onto his hands and knees and went scuttling into a corner— the one farthest from the door.

'Well,' Old Scratch rasped. 'It lives. And it moves. Frizzle, this is Jack, who is to be a goatherd by and by. Jack, this is Frizzle Face. He has vowed himself to silence, so is no company at all, but the eggs he brings are welcome and he has the ear of our Lord, so be good and show respect.'

*Respect be hanged. Respect be fried in a dirty pan and thrown to the crows.*

Jack hunkered lower on the balls of his feet. As soon as the bad thought about pans and crows had gone, he scowled at the young man from the monastery. And Frizzle Face (whose real name was Thomas Day) looked back at him calmly enough— charitably, even—although the short hairs on the nape of his neck felt suddenly sharp, and the voice he had vowed never to use again, except in the chanting of sacred songs, had come fluttering up in his throat, forcing him to gulp and swallow.

'I'm going to coddle you an egg,' Old Scratch was telling Jack. 'And you'll eat it, every shred, or I'll get Frizzle here to take you with him when he goes. The holy men can have you, and good luck to them . . .'

In the seethe and tumult of his mind, Jack pictured men with holes right through them, walking around like sieves on legs. It seemed quite monstrous to him that such men should exist. He knew—just knew— that he would detest those men on sight and that they, in turn, would think precious little of him.

Frizzle . . .

*Sounds like 'sizzle' don't it my sweet? Would you like to watch him burn, hmmm?*

Jack blinked He always blinked when bad thoughts came into his head. He didn't know why he had them—his Ja never did—nor did he always understand what they meant. All he knew—all he remembered—was that they made him want to hurt people. Had he? Was that why he was in this place, with a crooked old man and the Frizzle? Had he been sent here for being bad?

His head was a whirl. He could barely think. Barely remember . . .

A bird. He had hurt a bird, once. Or had he? And when? It seemed like a night-thought now, this faint, strange memory of shooing a bird down a garden path. Of getting angrier and angrier because it wouldn't fly away, and then . . . and then . . . the birdie had stopped moving altogether, and he had been glad, although he hadn't stomped on it—had he?—or done more—surely?—than wish it ill.

And, now, this person, this good Frizzle who brought eggs but never spoke . . . Jack was aware of wanting to hurt him, badly, the way he had hurt the bird. He was too exhausted, though, to think any more on it. Too weak from lack of sustenance, and from pining for his Ja.

*Ja. Oh, my good Ja. Where?*

The absence of Janet hit him so hard, then, that he crumpled; toppling the short distance backwards to sit, hard, upon the floor. Clumsily, he pressed his fists against his eyes to stop the strange, molten, melting that he knew, from watching Janet, was called crying.

'Well then . . .' Old Scratch hobbled across the shack, holding out a mess of egg on a spare plate, sliced from a log. 'Will you be good?'

Jack did not look up, nor did he speak. But one of his fists became an outstretched hand, and he took the piece of log, with egg on it, and began, very slowly, to eat.

'All right,' Old Scratch conceded. 'It's a start. It'll do, for now, won't it Frizzle? The eating, I mean. The perking up.'

Thomas Day made a slight movement of his head; somewhere between a yes, out of politeness, and a no for honesty. Because if perking up and eating a bit of egg meant that this boy was going to live and thrive, then nowhere could he find it, in his usually kind and loving heart, to be glad. *Why not?* he wondered. *What is it about this child that repels me so?*

Backing out of the shack, Thomas felt the sun hot on the place where his neck hairs had risen and, for the first time in all his sixteen years on earth, felt touched by something that might not, after all, be Heaven-blessed. For his neck did not feel kissed, as it usually did by the sun, but blasted as if by the heat from some furnace. And the child was to blame. As strange and impossible as it seemed, the child was affecting, if not the sun itself, then the way that he, Thomas Day, perceived it.

And that was a scary thing. A scary, *unnatural* thing.

Neither Jack nor Old Scratch said farewell as their visitor hastened away. Jack was too busy finishing his food; Old Scratch too busy watching him eat.

'All right,' the old man said, as Jack lifted the slice of log and began to lick it properly clean. 'All right, Jack the Lad, that'll do. Stop now, or you'll splinter your tongue.' He took the slice of log away. 'Now drink some milk,' he said. 'And we'll start again shall we, you and I? You learn to look after my goats and I'll learn to look after you. We'll both make mistakes, I'm thinking, but we'll rub along all right in time. So . . . will you be good? Do you understand that much, at least?'

Jack did. And, with the greatest reluctance, he nodded. Until he could make better sense of where he was, and why, it seemed the most sensible thing for him to do. He pictured his Ja—her sweet face more familiar to him than his own—and felt her absence, once again, as an all-through, all-over ache. Then, seeing no other choice for himself, at that point in time, he buried the hurt somewhere deep in his being. Where it grew.

*Where am I? Where? And what is 'dead'? And where is my Ja? I am Jack the Lad, the Old Man says. I will be a goatherd by and by. I eat my food. I drink my drink. I wait to understand.*

*Ja . . . my good Ja . . . I dream . . . I dream of you. We are almost six, you and I. I can milk a* goat. Can you milk a goat? You'd be gentler than me. I dig my nails in, on purpose, to make those goaties skitter and bleat. You would chastise me for that and I would stop. Without you, I do not stop. Without you, I am all bad. The bad Ja.

Sometimes I sleep in the goat shack, rolled all around in straw. I was born in there, the Old Man says, so little wonder that I feel a pull to go back, late, late at night, to goaty smells, and goaty sounds and, sometimes, the dribbly scratch of a goaty-tongue on my fast-asleep face. It is where I belong, the Old Man says, but he is a stupid stinker. I belong with you.

Eight. We are eight now. I think to run away, to look for you wherever you may be, but the holey men are watching, the Old Man says. The holey men catch runaway boys and lock them up for ever. I am not afraid of the holey men—I am not afraid of anyone—but if I am locked up for ever I will never see you again, and that I will not risk.

There is a bench, where you are, made out of stone. Your eyes are very blue. Where are you? Far, far away, the Old Man says. Where, exactly? I ask. By which city or meadow or shore? He says he knoweth not; that he had never cared enough to ask when a travelling man—a stranger—took me to be a companion for you, his baby girl.

Then how knoweth you, I say, that it is far, far away? 'Because,' he tells me, 'the travelling man would have returned you sooner—ill-tempered little whelp that you are—had the journey not been tortuous and very, very long.'

The travelling man is a blur in my mind, like a man made out of mist. I remember, I think, a woman. Your mother? His wife? Annie. Yes . . . Annie is her name but she too is ill-formed. Only you, my good Ja, come bright and clear to me whenever I think of you which is most—all—of the time.

After two more moons have passed we will be ten. The Old Man says I should forget all about you, just as you, by now, will have quite forgotten me. I could kill the Old Man sometimes. I could wring his scrawny neck, only then I would starve (not straightaway, but eventually, after I'd roasted all the goats).

I badger the Old Man. I make him trawl his wits. That stranger, I say to him, the one who took me from this place and then brought me back again, what family name did he go by? His first name is Sam, I remember that much, but Sam what? Think, Old Man, think.

It escapes me, the Old Man replies. But it may have been Smith. Yes, I do believe it was Smith.

Looking for you, the Old Man says, would be

*like searching for a lost tooth in a forest. More
chance, he says, of finding the rainbow's end or
of stumbling upon a unicorn up in the goat shack.
One day, though, I will go from this place and not
rest until I have found you. One day, when I am
bigger, I will search the length and breadth of this
land for you, and neither the holey men nor any
other man will stop me, this I swear.*

*I am a big boy now. Eleven. And I rage, my Ja.
I rage. The Old Man is a-feared of me. Goats
no longer dare to lick my face, lest I grab their
slobbering tongues and rip them clean up from
their throats. The rage comes out of nowhere, so
that I must pound the ground with my fists, or
run as if my heels are on fire, up hill and down
dale, until the fury goes. I chop wood, imagining
necks. The chirruping of small birds is all babble
and irritation. I net them for pies—whole flocks
at a time—and crunch their tiny bones.*

*We shared a spoon, you and I. In my dreams
we share it still. One for Janet, one for Jack, the
old brown cart goes clacketty clack. Curds and
whey and our own shared spit . . . I taste this, in
my dreams, and wake up drooling.*

*I will find you; I WILL, though there be no
trail to follow, of pebbles, or breadcrumbs, or
anything else. I will find you, but must bide my
time some more.*

When I am sixteen, the Old Man says, he has a thing of great value for me, that belonged to the person who bore me. Give it to me now, I commanded, when he first told me of this thing, or I will slit your throat.

But, 'Ha!' he said. 'Slit away. Do your worst. Sixteen I said, and sixteen it shall be. Until that day dawns, Jack the Lad, you'll keep working for me—if we can call your sorry efforts work. After, you may go where you will, and do as you please. Threaten or badger me further and I will sell the valuable thing myself and live like a Lord, high on the hog, while there is breath, still, in my body.'

At least tell me where it is, this thing, I wheedled, lest you drop down dead one of these fine days, leaving me without the knowledge and as poor, still, as a ditch-born mouse.

'Ha!' he said again. 'How big a fool do you take me for, young master? There is another who knows; an upright, honest cove who has sworn to do right by you, when the times comes, should I have gone to the ground. But only, mark you, if I be dead from natural causes: no mark of rope or fingers around my neck; no poison frothing my nostrils; no nasty bump upon my head. And he'd check. Don't imagine that he wouldn't. He would examine my poor old corpse, most thoroughly, for signs of foul play, and know full well who to blame should he find any.'

*Then beware unfortunate accidents, Old Man,*
*I raged at him. Walk ye not in any forest, on a*
*wild and windy morn, lest a bough should fall*
*and crush your skull, leaving me to be called*
*murderer. Pick mushrooms and berries no more,*
*lest you mistake what is good for what will kill*
*you in a trice. And rile me not—keep out of my*
*way in fact, Old Man—for there are days when,*
*I swear, I know not what I do.*

*The 'upright, honest cove' the Old Man spoke*
*of is a lanky waste of skin called Thomas Day*
*who resides at the monastery, an hour's walk*
*from here. He used to bring eggs, when I was*
*young, then he went away, and I was glad. Good*
*riddance, I thought, and worse. But he returned,*
*damn his eyes, the summer before last as a holey*
*man full-fledged. His head is stuffed with tish*
*and tosh from some scholarly place or other, and*
*he has found his stupid tongue, not that I have*
*heard him use it, for he cometh not out here, the*
*Old Man goes to him. Brother Day is civilized*
*company, he says, and a pleasure to be with,*
*inferring, of course, that I, myself, am not.*

*I used to think, my Ja, that you could see*
*daylight through the holey men. I imagined them*
*punched through by shots such as a very small*
*cannon might fire, yet living still and breathing,*
*after a fashion.*

*I know better now.*

*How tediously the weeks do pass, how achingly slow the months. How I seethe and long to go; to find my good Ja, wherever she may be. I try to count the hours until I turn sixteen, but they are beyond my reckoning.*

*We are twelve now. Bad thoughts fill my head, until it is a mucky place. You used to take my hand, Ja, when my head filled so, and the bad thoughts would fade. You banished them. Those thoughts were nothing compared to what swirls in my head these days. It is only by remembering the touch of your hand and the murmur of your voice, that I am able, after much torment and struggle, to think clearly once again.*

*Do I see you as you were? No. I see you as you are. Tall for a girl—as tall as I, perhaps—your skin so pale that your hand in mine would glimmer. Your eyes are kind, still, and as blue as the sky can be in springtime. And your hair though darker now (more wheat than barley-coloured) is as fine, still, as fairy-thread; so fine it goes to tangles in the slightest breeze and you dread the tug of a comb more than anything.*

*Many moons have passed, Ja, since last I spoke your name. I conjure your image in secret, lest the Old Man mock me for a deluded ninny. He has never understood—will never understand— that you and I belong together, like two halves of a thing, and that somewhere you have been waiting—are waiting still—for the day when I will find you.*

*Soon, my Ja, soon. We are a month off fourteen. My voice is a man's. I am strong. I go to the market now, with the Old Man. He has become too stooped and twisted to pull the cart alone. Get a horse, you tight-fisted old sot, I rage at him, but he says he hasn't the means. We will buy one between us, he tells me, when we have made our fortune selling cheese. Hah! say I. Dream on, Old Man . . .*

*The first time I went to the market I fair shivered from the shock of it. People, Ja. I am not so used to people. Women, in particular, gave me much pause for thought. The brightness of them . . . the scent and sound of them . . . the way they dimpled and smiled at me as they flocked around the cart. We sold a lot of cheese that day. 'You're good for business, Jack the Lad,' the Old Man said and bought for me a fiddle. 'What?' I said. 'Are you going soft, Old Man? Are you losing what's left of your wits along with the strength in both legs and all the hairs on your pate?' 'Take it,' he replied. 'And be grateful, you little whelp.'*

*I go alone, now, to the market, to sell, and to watch the people. There is only one face I* want—nay, long—to see, but I must continue to wait, I know, until I have the means to travel, for as long, and as far as I must.

And presents. I will want to buy you presents. Ribbons and kittens and shoes of Spanish leather. I keep a goodly share of the cheese money, to add to my inheritance. The Old Man calls me a thankless, thieving cove but I remind him that I . . . I am good for business, while he is a shambling old crock; no more capable of selling a cheese these days than of running up Glastonbury Tor.

I ask folk at the market: 'Do you remember . . . can you recall . . . a travelling man who passed this way fifteen winters ago? A man by the name of Sam? Sam Smith, perhaps?' It is a long shot. They shake their heads. The women grow impertinent: 'Was he your father, young master?' they wonder. 'If so, he must have been a handsome cove. We would have remembered a travelling man with a look of you about him. We would have persuaded "Sam-Smith-perhaps" to stay awhile, and would have fought like cats for his favours.'

Such teasing makes my blood boil, so I ask no more. Perhaps, one day, I will spy the one who did sell the Old Man my fiddle. A gipsy, by the look of him, the Old Man has said (for I myself did not see the cove). A man in a hooded cloak, who had a beard such as a goat does sport, and eyes reddened by dust, or exhaustion, or some deep and private sorrow.

One travelling man might know of another. At least that's what I hope. But he who sold the fiddle has yet to pass this way again.

Your father's name is Sam, of that I remain quite sure. And your mother is Annie. Sam, Annie and Janet Smith. In a good-sized house, with gardens front and back, a stone bench and . . . I'm fairly certain . . . beehives. Yes. Beehives. You had a few of those. I will travel north first, then south, then east, then west, until I find this place or someone who knows of it, and of you and Sam and Annie, and can point me out the way.

Soon, now, my Ja. Very, very soon.

# XI

Old Scratch thought less and less, as time went by, about the ring with the blood-coloured stone in it. Having dangled the idea of great riches in front of young Jack, the way a farmer might have dangled a carrot before the eyes of a work-shy donkey, he had decided not to lose any sleep over what the boy would surely do when he turned sixteen and found his 'thing of great value' to be worth little more than a cheese.

And that lie he'd told, about the young monk, Frizzle Face, knowing all there was to know. What if that came back to bite him? Again, he had decided just to let the matter lie.

Jack's sixteenth birthday had, after all, seemed a very long way off when the valuable thing was first mooted. *I could be in the ground by then*, Old Scratch had told himself. *Or the boy might have settled . . . might have come to love the goats as much as I do, and to care more about living quietly, here with me, than heading into the great unknown with a fortune to piss away.*

And my goats might fly, he could have added. Or the moon turn to honeycomb the next time it wanes.

Playing safe, Old Scratch had taken the ring out of its hiding place, in the hollow log, wrapped it in a bladder and hidden it somewhere better—half a foot beneath the ground, six paces from the shack. *I'll worry about it nearer the time*, he had thought, thumping a square of turf back into place.

The time grew nearer.

And nearer still.

Jack was doing well at the market; charming the ladies and selling so much cheese that the goats were having trouble keeping up. He tended the herd (some thirty strong now) without complaint and, at night, he played the fiddle . . . played it with such verve and skill that Old Scratch couldn't help but tap his feet and nod along, amazed.

It had been months—years—since the thing of great value had been spoken of by either of them. As for the Huckles, Old Scratch had seen nothing of Sam since the night Jack had been returned, nor had he heard, or tried to find out, how Sam and his family fared.

Jack's fifteenth birthday had been, as usual, unseasonably warm. The boy had joked, and even sung, as he went about his chores and a smile had danced on his lips, that night, as he played a bold jig on his fiddle. *One more year*, he'd been thinking, his spirits leaping in time with the bow. *Just one more year to go . . .*

*He's settled*, Old Scratch had concluded, on the strength of the smile and the jig. *He won't be going anywhere.* And the ring with the blood-coloured stone in it could have been nosed away by moles, and the Huckles re-settled a hundred miles away for all the thought Scratch gave to them after that.

# XII

Jack heard the rumour from a gossip at the market, who had heard it from her husband, who had heard it in the tavern from a man whose son always kept his ears well-pricked and had heard it while delivering a barrel of eels to the monastery kitchen.

'Those monks could leave at any time,' the woman informed Jack, bending low over an arrangement of cheeses, to whisper in his ear. 'In broad daylight, should they want to make a point; or by dead of night if they're planning to haul away their precious things before the King's men go storming in, to claim the merry lot.'

'What precious things?' Jack wanted to know. 'They live in poverty don't they, the holey men? They give everything up, eat sparingly, if at all, and wear hair shirts to give themselves sores which fester and don't look pretty.'

The woman straightened up, and rolled her eyes in mock despair. 'Which nest did you tumble out of, young master?' she teased. 'To be so ill-versed in the true ways of the world?'

Jack scowled. He hated to be teased. And this woman—this fat old gossip—was testing his patience and diluting his charm. 'I'm right about the shirts,' he told her, tersely. 'The Old Man makes them out of goats' hair. He used to deliver them personally, and return with beans and ale.'

The woman shook her head at him and smiled a tolerant smile. 'That doesn't mean,' she said, as if to a dim-wit or a child of four, 'that they were ever worn.'

This exchange left Jack out of sorts. The old gossip had been right, he had to admit it. He *was* ill-versed: as ignorant as a pig in muck about matters outside his own small experience. Would his Ja, he wondered, suddenly, think him ignorant? Enough to want to shun him? The very idea made his skin prickle and his mouth go dry He had never considered such a thing before, never worried at all about any trait or circumstance which might make his and Janet's reunion anything less than perfect.

Self-doubt was new to Jack the Lad. He could not—would not—give in to it.

## Quite right too, my sweet. You are who you are. Walk tall.

Jack blinked. The gossip was ambling away. Jack watched her go, noting the casual swing of her hips, and the way her basket jounced against her side, as if she might be chortling. Staring, angrily, at the back of her head, he imagined he could see right through it, to where her fat-woman thoughts bubbled and teemed. She was planning, he felt certain, to tell her husband, who would tell the man in the tavern, who would tell his son, who would tell the saints only knew who else, that Old Scratch's boy was a cloth-witted fool, fit more for display than purpose.

'Blasts and fogs upon thee,' he muttered. 'You waggle-tongued crone! You Queen of sour curds!'

When she stumbled and fell, he was glad. He knew he ought not to be, but he was. *Serves you right*, he thought, *for crossing Jack the Lad.* There were others around to haul her to her feet; to commiserate with her over her twisted ankle and ruined stockings, and to pick up the apples that had spilled from her basket and were rolling in the dirt, like the heads of little traitors.

'Who tripped me?' the woman hollered, leaning heavily on the ones who had hauled her up. 'Someone did. Someone kicked my left foot right out from under me, and now, I swear, it feels like a lump of lead. Who was it, neighbours? I need witnesses. There'll be a bruise on me, tomorrow, the size of Salisbury.'

But: 'You just cockled over, Kate Bundy,' a fellow-gossip informed her. 'No one tripped you—there was no one near. Your bones must have had a weak moment. It happens.'

Jack had already turned away. He couldn't care less what had caused his tormentor to fall. She was a fat, wobbly thing who had probably tripped over her own swollen feet.

He began to pack away his unsold cheeses. It was too early for him to be leaving the market, but there was somewhere else he needed to be: somewhere he had sworn to avoid, for as long as he lived, but felt compelled, now, to go to. Immediately. Without delay. Because never mind what precious things the holey men might be planning to disappear with; he had his own thing of value to think about and protect. And, with the Old Man so ancient now that he could meet his maker any day, there was one particular holey man who was going nowhere until he, Jack the Lad, had been told the precise whereabouts of his inheritance.

# XIII

Brother Day was down on his knees, weeding a herb bed and praying for guidance. Should he stay or should he go? He had his eyes closed as he felt around the base of a rosemary bush for things to root up and get rid of. His shirt, as he moved, was chafing fresh blisters across the rubbed-raw blades of his shoulders.

He didn't want to leave the monastery. Where, after all, would he go? He was too young to be pensioned off like all the other monks and, unlike them, had no nephew, cousin, or Very Important Associate to escape to, and no sanctuary to head for, beyond the monastery gates. But if he stayed, what then? The way he saw it, there would be two—no, three—paths open to him:

One: he could swear allegiance to King Henry, and the new Church of England, and continue on as a priest.

Two: he could leave the Church to lead, instead, the life of an ordinary man; a simple God-fearing man with a wife, perhaps, and children, to sweeten his time on earth.

Three: he could rebel. Join, or even lead, an uprising. Refuse to accept the King's right to dabble in religious affairs and never mind the consequences, which would, he knew, be dire.

Choices, choices . . .

*Lord*, he prayed, leaning back on his heels. *Send me a sign. Send one now, this very minute, that I may recognize it, and know what I must do.*

Ever hopeful, he opened his eyes. Through slants of April sunshine, he saw something flicker, in the pear tree that grew some thirty strides away against the garden wall.

*Dragonfly, bird or angel?* It was probably a bird, he told himself; a little bird, pick-pecking at the blossom. Still, he closed his eyes again, and made himself be still, just in case . . . on the marvellous off chance that whatever was up in that pear tree might expand . . . grow . . . materialize, to stand before him with strict instructions . . . good advice . . . a clue.

'Brother Thomas?'

He gasped, amazed.

*An angel? It had to be, for the voice . . . that voice had not been of this world, and his name had sounded extraordinary, as if newly bestowed.*

'Yes?' he whispered. 'I'm listening.'

He kept his eyes tight shut, afraid to have them scorched by too much dazzle and glory. Bending lower—so low that his nose and forehead hit the soil—he willed his limbs not to tremble. They trembled anyway. Which path, he dared to wonder, was he about to be assigned by this . . . this messenger from on high? How he dreaded being sent along the third one. The road to rebellion. The route that would surely see him hanged, drawn and quartered before the first frosts. Yet how he thrilled, too, to think of it. The purity of the cause. The *rightness* of it . . .

Was he brave enough, then, to die a martyr of the Holy Roman Church, like the Abbot of Glastonbury and all those others? He had to admit that he was not. Not unless whoever . . . whatever . . . stood before him now told him it had to be so. For then he would know, with utter certainty, that the death of a righteous man was not a prelude to nothing at all but a tumble into eternal bliss. And if he was destined to see his own innards steaming on the tip of a poker, that would definitely be a thing worth knowing in advance.

Hardly daring to breath, he prepared to accept his fate. In his heart of hearts he realized, sadly, he wanted a quiet life.

'There is someone here to see you, Brother Thomas. Old Scratch's boy. The foundling.'

*What?*

With a jerk of his head, Thomas took in the sight of Brother Francis, more scarecrow than celestial being in his threadbare robe and soft-soled slippers. All monks moved so quietly, like shadows across stone and grass. He should have realized. Should have guessed. *You simpleton*, he chided himself. *You ninny.*

'Old Scratch's boy,' Brother Francis rasped, 'is in the lane outside. He won't come any closer, but it's you he wants to see. On a matter of great importance he said.'

This was the longest string of words to have come out of Brother Francis in more than thirty years. He had intended his vow of silence to last as long as he did but, with the monastery about to be closed, and its inhabitants shooed away, like weevils from a biscuit, he had changed his mind and begun, in dribs and drabs, to speak. 'Lord,' he had said first, followed by, 'Forgive' and then, 'Me'. 'My slippers are falling apart,' he had said, since then, and, 'I would like roast pheasant for my lunch, please, and a cup or two of mead.'

His voice was odd from lack of use; not an angel's, though, and Thomas didn't know whether to feel cheated or relieved. His own voice hadn't croaked like that, when he had decided, after not very much soul-searching, to start using it again. But then, he hadn't kept quiet for anywhere near as long as Brother Francis. And he had never stopped singing—the monastery's need for a boy soprano had been too great for that.

Rising to his feet; aware of the need to concentrate fully, now, on mundane and earthly matters, Thomas trawled his memory for the name of Old Scratch's boy. He must be—what? —fourteen, fifteen by now? Recalling an odd, unlikeable child, Thomas wondered vaguely what kind of youth would be waiting for him outside the monastery gates. He would have come about Old Scratch, of that much Thomas was certain.

The old goatherd was probably dying, or had already passed. The boy might want a candle lit, and prayers said. He might even have brought the means to pay for it. And that—he allowed himself a tiny smile—really would be a miracle.

Jack had left the cart, and his unsold cheeses, in a ditch. He didn't care what became of them. If they were still there in a bit, fine. If not, to blazes with them. He wanted to stand before Brother Frizzle Face Day man to man, not lowly ill-versed cheese seller before holey person-on-high.

Being outside the monastery was making him feel odd. Tired and a little bit sick. He recognized Day as soon as he saw him and leapt across the lane, eager to get the business between the two of them sorted and out of the way.

'Where is it?' he shouted. 'My inheritance. My thing of value. Tell me. I need to know.'

Thomas stopped walking and considered the question. After a while, he shook his head. 'I can't help you,' he said, pressing his hands together, palm to palm, as if a prayer, though interrupted, was still the main thing on his mind. 'I don't know what you're talking about.'

Jack squirmed. His own palms began to itch. He rubbed them on the seat of his trousers. 'Isn't it a sin to lie?' he hissed.

'It is,' Thomas agreed, keeping his voice beautifully calm. 'And I'm not.'

Jack swallowed, hard. Then he blinked. Brother

Day was taller than he was but scrawnier, he could tell, beneath that holey robe of his: a man with no might or muscle to him, and the pink and white complexion of a milk-fed girl. It had to be eight, maybe nine years, since they had last crossed paths. Brother Day hadn't been speaking then; had only handed Old Scratch a bag of eggs as if bestowing some kind of an honour, but Jack remembered the look on his frizzly face that time, and the same one was on it now: open, honest and so very, very smug that the temptation to slice it off with the knife he used for paring cheese was huge.

**Frizzle. Sounds like sizzle. If you're lying, wretch, we will rip the wisps from that chinny chin chin of yours and stuff them down your throat . . .**

But Brother Day, Jack could tell, would hold a finger over a candle flame until his flesh dripped rather than tell a lie. And it came to him, in a boiling rush, that Old Scratch was the villain in this affair; a lying scullion, with a lot of explaining to do.

'Right,' he said, blinking rapidly. 'We'll leave it at that.' He turned on his heel, unable to bear the sight of Thomas Day's goodness a moment longer. 'Good to talk to you,' he called back over his shoulder. 'Although I have to say, I'm puzzled. Aren't those vows you all take supposed to be for life?'

Troubled, Thomas watched Jack lope away. For no reason he could fathom, he sensed he had got off lightly. That, had the boy not been distracted by some nonsense about an inheritance (as if *that* was likely), a blow might have been struck, there in the lane—a blade pulled, even—and he, Thomas Day, would have had more pain to contend with than had ever been caused by the wearing of a goats' hair shirt.

As it was, he felt worn out by their encounter. Almost too tired to move. And—he thumped his chest and cleared his throat—his insides felt all scratched about, as if he had breathed in grit or swallowed a piece of his shirt.

That foundling, he mused—what *was* his name?—had not, after all, improved with age. There was gipsy blood in him, Old Scratch had said, and a temper that could strike sparks in pouring rain.

He coughed, again, and spat. Little bits of something solid flew out of his mouth with his spittle. Odd, he thought, wiping his lips with the back of one hand. And worrying. Then he remembered: earlier, when he'd bowed to Brother Francis, his face had gone smack into the herb bed, had it not? *Fool*, he thought. *You swallowed dirt.*

Three times more he coughed and spat before starting to feel better. Scratch's boy, he was glad to note, had disappeared along the lane.

*If I don't see him again for another ten years it will be too soon*, Thomas thought. *He puzzles me. No—he scares me.*

# XIV

Jack clenched his fists and aimed a kick at a tussock of grass. Just heading towards the shack (he would not call it home—had never called it home) was fuelling his already white-hot rage. If he didn't simmer down—just a little, just enough—before confronting the Old Man, he would pulverize the treacherous old gut-bag on sight, no questions asked or reasons given, and then might never know where his thing of great value had been hidden (if it existed, which it better had, otherwise . . .).

Too restless to stand still, while his temper cooled, he began walking aimlessly back towards the monastery. He half hoped Brother Day would still be dithering in the lane, so that he could smack him, just the once, in passing. But Brother Day was nowhere to be seen.

Nearing the gates, Jack broke into a run. The monastery repelled him. He ran from it as if from a beast: a tethered but ravenous monster, with a taste for hot-headed boys. He ran for many minutes and several miles, before slowing down. There were woods up ahead. Bluebell woods. He would go in there, he decided, and stomp around. Kill some time. Kill a squirrel if he saw one. Let off a bit more steam.

He waded in. There was a narrow path twisting this way and that but he ignored it. A low-hanging branch almost cracked him in the teeth. Furious, he ripped it from its tree, and began using it to thwack his own way through the wood. Bluebells buckled and snapped as he let swing at them with the branch, and their leaves and stalks squeaked, like creatures, as he trampled them underfoot. On and on he went, his boots sticky with sap, his anger leaking out of him in grunts and heartfelt curses: *Scratch, you lying old viper . . . Day, you puny, frizzle-faced, clod-hopping . . .*

Blundering into a clearing, he skidded, stopped and caught his breath. It was like stumbling upon a pool of scented water. Sunlight streamed, in long shafts, from a sky as blue as the flowers, and from somewhere away to his left, he heard a cuckoo call.

Jack was not insensitive to beauty. The loveliness of the clearing touched him—moved him, even— but he took no pleasure from it. For a long time now beautiful days, or scenes, or moments had made him feel slug-ugly by comparison. Not to look at (he was, he knew, exceptionally good to look at) but inside; in his head, in his heart, and in his soul, wherever that lived. And because he hated being made to feel this way he had got used to turning his back, or closing his eyes, or spoiling, if he could, the beauty of the day, or the scene, or the moment.

This was, he knew, a pitiful way to behave. But his Ja would sort him out. Once he and she were reunited, her goodness would rub off on him like pollen and he would begin to think better of himself and, in time, of everything else.

## More flowers? Rip 'em up.

Jack blinked. He was bored with destroying the bluebells. As a child of five or six he would have reduced the whole clearing to a mess of bruised, blue clots and then attacked a few trees for good measure. But he was fifteen years old now, for mercy's sake, and there was a limit to how much satisfaction he could get out of bluebell-bashing.

A new sound reached him: the steady thud of an axe. Further into the wood, someone was felling a tree.

## Go back and stamp on a 'holey man', then. Any 'holey man' will do. Stamp on his face, my sweet, until the slime on your boots is worth knowing about.

Jack flinched.
*What? WHAT?*

Bad thoughts no longer startled him. They were a fact of his life. But all the same . . .

## If everything else is child's play now, aim higher. Go dance a jig on a Holy Roman smile. Go on.

*That's vile*, Jack managed to think. *And a hanging offence*. And yet . . . there was certainly one face he would like to rearrange. One smile he would probably take pleasure in spoiling with a few well-aimed kicks.

### So, go.

Halfway round, Jack turned, before a fresh thought came into his head: CHILD? BE STILL. YOU HAVE A CHOICE. And it was as if a sunbeam had entered his right ear while poison flooded the left.

Confused, he shook his head; shook it savagely, from side to side. When he stopped, his mind was clear. Relieved, he breathed in the bluebell-scent, and waited for his heart to slow.

The bad thoughts, he had to admit, were getting worse. Had been for a while. And for the first time ever he wondered: *Do they grow in my head like toadstools? Or* . . . turning back to the clearing he looked, warily, up at the sky, . . . *are they being put there? And, if they are being put there who . . . or what . . . is doing this to me?*

Feeling exposed—vulnerable—he stepped backwards, into deep shade. Still he continued to watch the sky. *And another thing*, he thought. *Where did that other voice come from? The one that called me 'Child'?* Like Thomas Day, he wanted a sign. Unlike Thomas Day, he didn't feel on good enough terms with God to ask for one.

Unworthy. That's how Jack the Lad felt. With the scent of bluebells coming at him in waves, and the cuckoo's song and the thud of the woodcutter's axe filling his ears like sunbeams and poison, he knew himself to be an ill-versed, foul-tempered waste of skin, with no friends, no prospects, no good Ja (yet) and—probably—no inheritance.

The tears that filled his eyes felt horrible. He hadn't cried since he was three. It hurt to cry.

## Pull yourself together, you mewling little puke. You have work to do. It's time.

*Time for what. TIME FOR WHAT?*

And then he heard another voice, only not in is his head this time. A girl's voice, high and clear, winding through the trees.

'Catch the ball, Dorigan. Here it comes. You can do it.'

*Just a foolish maid*, he thought, although his pulse had quickened, again, and his face turned to the sound, as if pulled by a string. *No one you need bother about, unless she comes a-bothering you.*

The girl's voice pealed once more, even closer this time: 'Again, butter fingers, try again!' No longer a child's but not quite a woman's, it could only belong to a stranger. And yet . . .

Deep in Jack's being, something shifted.

# XV

The sisters burst, like dryads, into the clearing. They didn't notice Jack as they began, with little shrieks and giggles, and a lot of flailing around, to leap from one tree stump to another.

'Your turn,' the younger girl called out, throwing a red-painted ball. But her sister had reached a particular stump in the very middle of the clearing and was standing on tiptoe on it, her arms raised and her fingers fluttering skywards, as if she might catch and hold fast to the sun.

*Lovely*, she was thinking. *The day is lovely. The flowers are lovely. I want to fly . . .*

The ball dropped among the bluebells, like a great big berry, and the younger girl stamped her foot. 'You're worse than any butter fingers,' she scolded. 'You've stopped playing without *telling* me. You're not supposed to do that. I hate it when you do that. And now the ball needs finding, so the jump-game is spoiled as well.' Carefully, she stepped in among the bluebells. 'Where did it go? I didn't hear where it . . . *oh*!'

Her hands flew to her mouth, holding in a scream. Jack ignored her. His gaze was fixed on the older girl, who, spotlit by a sunbeam, and completely self-absorbed, had begun, very slowly, to dance.

She was tall and pale and her long, wheat-coloured hair had gone to tangles in the breeze.

'Ja,' Jack whispered. 'My Ja . . .'

The younger girl was scrambling now, scrambling, and falling, then scrambling again; knee-deep in bluebells; hitting out at them and missing.

'Dorigan—whatever's wrong?'

Jack thought his heart was going to burst from the bones of his chest. Burst out, fly through the air, and then land somewhere, like a gory valentine. He couldn't speak. He couldn't move. And all he could think when finally . . . at last . . . the dancing girl looked his way was, *My Ja . . . my Ja . . . my Ja . . .*

'If you come any closer,' the girl said to him, 'I will call for help. That's our father you can hear, chopping wood, and he's a fast runner.'

Jack blinked. He was, he realized, still holding the torn-off branch, holding it tight in both fists, and half-raised, like a weapon. It was enough, he supposed, to frighten any girl. Dropping it, he found his voice:

'Ja,' he rasped, reaching out with his empty hands. 'It's me.' He wanted to run to her. He wanted to lift her off that tree stump and whirl her round and round and round. He wanted to pull her to the ground and lie there with her; cradled by flower stalks; breathing her in. He wanted time to stand still, and the lumpy little sister to disappear, and everything to be perfect, from this moment on, for him and for his Ja.

Because it *was* her. No doubt or question. He would have known her anywhere. She was his Ja, and she was *right there in front of him*, and why he hadn't collapsed, or even died, from the thrill of it was both a miracle and a blessing.

'It's me,' he repeated, taking one . . . two . . . steps into the clearing. 'It really is, Ja. It's *me*.'

But the girl on the tree stump was staring at him as if he might be mad. And her sister had taken refuge behind her and was peeping round, afraid.

'Stop! Don't move, I said. Weren't you listening? Take one more step and I'll scream. We both will.'

Confused, Jack stopped and let his hands fall, useless, to his sides. He felt—what?—something like anger but colder, and more frightening, rising in his gut.

'But . . . *I'm your Ja*,' he insisted. 'Remember?' He heard, and regretted, the impatience in his voice; the pig-squeal of frustration.

'Ja,' the older girl repeated, and it just sounded odd.

Jack took a deep, steadying breath. **Don't get angry** he told himself. **Don't frighten her**. His next words, he knew, had to be absolutely right. They had to touch a chord. She should have known him straightaway, but she hadn't. He should be spilling his thoughts all over her—years of yearning, and waiting, and hoping, being spoken aloud, at last. But that wasn't going to happen. Not yet.

'Your father's name is Sam,' he said. 'And your mother is Annie. We shared a cradle, you and I, and a spoon. *One for Janet, one for Jack. The old brown cart goes clacketty clack.*' He kept his tone polite as he measured each word, like sugar from a bag.

When she frowned, trying to remember, he risked a smile. It was the kind of smile he might have bestowed upon a pretty girl at the market, to get her to come over to him and buy a bit of cheese.

'You used to hold my hand,' he continued, carefully. 'When I felt . . . under the weather. We were inseparable, you and I.' *Are inseparable*, he reminded himself. *We* ARE *inseparable, Ja. I just need you to remember.*

Janet Huckle studied him coolly. He wanted to take that pretty face of hers between both his hands and gaze at it until extreme hunger, intolerable thirst or an overwhelming need for sleep forced him to take a break. Not moving any further towards her was insufferable. Not moving was requiring more willpower, and patience, than he had endured in twelve years of waiting for this moment to arrive.

'I remember . . .' he eventually heard her say, 'making dumplings. Yes, that's right. There was a boy who used to make dumplings with me. Was that you?'

'Yes.'

'I *thought* so. The dough was too sticky and the spoon too big for me to stir all by myself. Oh, and I remember . . . I *think* I remember . . . when I wanted to dance, when I was really very little, you used to try and stop me. You used to sit on my feet, if mother wasn't looking, or . . . or *growl*. Am I right?'

He paused. 'Yes.'

She clapped her hands, pleased with herself. 'It's all right Dorigan,' she said, looking fondly down at the top of her sister's head. 'This person means us no harm. He remembers father, and mother, and I from a long time ago. From before you were born. His name is . . . ?' she looked expectantly across the clearing.

'Jack.'

'Jack,' she repeated. 'Well, master Jack, do you want to say hello to father? He will remember you, I'm sure. Dorigan and I will go and fetch him . . .'

'No!' Jack clenched his fists, then hid them behind his back. 'You stay here. Send the child.' Keeping calm was killing him. Keeping calm was not something he had felt inclined to practise, down the years. 'Please,' he added, in a better voice. 'You stay.'

Janet reached for the younger girl's hand. 'My sister cannot see,' she said. 'Not well enough, anyway, to go wandering through these woods all by herself.'

Jack spared the nuisance child a glance. How old was she—nine? Ten? She flinched and hid her face in both her hands. *Not so blind*, Jack thought, *that she can't tell when she's being looked at, and wished three counties away.* 'But you were playing catch,' he said petulantly. 'If she can catch a ball she can fetch your father, surely.'

Janet raised her eyebrows. Who are you, said the expression on her face, to have any idea at all about how my sister sees the world?

'All right,' Jack said quickly. 'All right, I'm sorry.'
*Be careful. Don't rile her. Think . . . think . . .*

He was reminded of netting songbirds. There was an art to it; a way of creeping up on the bush they were in, without startling them into flight. You had to move with infinite care and patience. One false step, or sound, and they were gone.

He blinked, and then he bowed—a grand and courtly gesture, which he hoped would make up for any clumsy remarks. And for earlier, when she'd seen him brandishing a branch and acting crazy, from the shock.

'It's been a pleasure, girls,' he said. 'But now I have to go. My guardian is elderly, and not long for this world. I must hurry back, and see to him.'

'Really? Oh . . . well . . .'

*No, not really, Ja. Not really at all. I'd sooner chop off my own feet than walk away from you but you . . . are . . . being . . . so . . .*

'Well, that's a pity. Might we see you again?'

The thrill Jack felt, then, almost made him whoop. Never mind that irritating 'we'. His leaving was a pity! And she wanted to see him again!

*Slowly . . . slowly . . .*

'Maybe tomorrow,' he said, as if the following day was a dull place where whatever chanced to happen would only make him yawn. 'I could meet you here again tomorrow, I suppose. Earlier than this, though—before noon?'

Janet nodded.

'All right,' she said. 'And perhaps you will come home with us tomorrow, to say hello to mother and take a cup of ale with father?'

Jack blinked. Too many people. Too many unwanted, bothersome people. He left the invitation hanging, and tried another smile. This time, Janet Huckle smiled back.

'You used to hide under our table, didn't you?' she said. 'You used to dive under there, with a face like a winter Monday, and refuse to come out. You were a bit of a cross patch, master Jack, if I remember rightly.'

'A bit,' he agreed. 'But I would cheer up, soon enough, for you. Only for you, mind, no one else. You were the sweetest thing. You still are.'

He watched the blush colour her face and knew—just knew—that he had her. He might have danced, then, for joy, and for the first time in his life, but:

'I'll see you tomorrow, Janet Smith,' he said, turning away. 'Huckle,' she corrected him. 'It's Janet Huckle.'

He looked back.

'Of course it is. And your father, Sam. Good old Sam Huckle—is he still a travelling man?'

Janet shook her head. 'My father is a carpenter.'

'Uh-huh,' Jack said. 'Sorry. Memory like a sifter. So . . . your house. I'm picturing gardens, back and front . . . a stone bench . . . beehives . . . it must be . . . somewhere close?'

'Oh, very.' Letting go her sister's hand, Janet pointed, cheerfully, through the trees. 'It's over there, about a minute's walk along the lane.'

'Well, well,' Jack managed, through the roaring in his head. 'We're practically neighbours.'

# XVI

Old Scratch saw Jack coming and tried to run. He'd been standing outside the shack, propped up on two sticks, wondering, *Is it spring or autumn, and where is the boy?*

The boy, when he appeared, was moving uncommonly fast. No cart. Raised fist. Feet pounding the lane like hooves. And then the yell: 'You're as good as dead, you lying scullion! You carcass fit for hounds!'

None of it boded well.

But running, along with controlling his bladder, and keeping track of his thoughts, was no longer something Old Scratch was any good at. Two painful, lurching, strides were all he managed before Jack was on him . . . kicking away his sticks . . . shaking him until he thought his eyes might burst like boiling berries, and his two remaining teeth go a-rattling down his gullet to peg down and puncture his lungs.

'She's JUST DOWN THE LANE. She's been there ALL THE TIME. And it's HUCKLE not SMITH. Did you know? Because if you knew . . .'

'No . . . I never . . . I swear . . .'

Jack tightened his grip on the old man's rags.

*Wring his neck.*

*I can't.*

*Oh but you can. And you should. You need the practice.*

*Go away.*

Old Scratch was choking. It would be so easy, Jack thought, to finish him off. The easiest thing in the world . . .

*So do it. Or petrify his sorry bones. You have the gift, my sweet. I'll help.*

*What? WHAT?*

Distracted, Jack lost his grip; considered tightening it again but found he hadn't the heart. 'ALL RIGHT,' he bellowed in the old man's ear. 'All right . . . But you're still a lying cur. WHERE IS IT?'

Feeling himself released, Old Scratch spluttered and reeled. Would his legs hold him up? Yes. Just. But his head . . . his poor old head . . . It felt so *heavy*; too heavy to lift. Could being yelled at do that to a head? For he hadn't been kicked, or walloped. He would have felt that. It would have hurt.

'Where's . . . what?' he wheezed, hanging his heavy head like a donkey. 'The cart? I don't . . . know . . .

dear boy . . . you had it last.' Without moving, he spat out a tooth.

'Not the cart, you botcher's apprentice. My inheritance. My thing of value.'

'Oh. That.'

Something had happened, Old Scratch realized. At the market. Something had occurred, or been said, and now the game was up.

'Belabour me no more,' he pleaded, raising both arms; protecting his head from any more of he knew not what. 'Leave me be, and I'll show you where I put it.'

It took forty minutes, and a lot of digging, before Jack found the ring with the blood coloured stone in it. 'Is this all there is?' he demanded, holding the ring up in the fast-fading light and squinting at the stone.

Old Scratch had retrieved his sticks and was dithering, and muttering, and worrying about his head, at what he hoped was a safe distance.

'Better than nothing,' he ventured. 'Better than a poke from the Devil's toasting fork.'

'What's it worth?'

'A lot, Jack, a lot. It belonged to your mother, and she was no hedge dweller.'

Jack, who at that point in time wouldn't have known gold from tin, or a ruby from a shard of bloodied glass, closed his fist around his inheritance, stood up, and barged into the shack. He took a blanket. He took his fiddle. He took all the cheese money he'd managed to save. And then, he took his leave.

'You can thank your lucky stars,' he bawled at Old Scratch, by way of a goodbye, 'that I didn't put you in the ground, in place of what is mine, and bang a dead-weight of turf down on your bones.'

Old Scratch coughed, and spat tooth-blood onto the ground. Both his ears were ringing and, still, he could not lift his head. 'Feels like I've a cannon ball a-swinging from my neck,' he said to his feet. 'Feels like I've a rock between my ears. Can't think why, for he didn't strike me. Got off lightly, Old Scratch did, in the end.'

And then the old man got to thinking . . . started trying to recall . . . there was something else, wasn't there, as well as that ring, that was the boy's, by rights? His mind snagged on the question, and then skittered away. He was remembering a January morning and that trudge through snow, with the boy, newborn, in his arms. He was hearing, again, bits of ill-tempered back chat . . . curses swapped, down all the years . . . and the sound of that fiddle, bringing what passed for wonder to his sorry old ears and flinty heart.

Something fluttered, on the edge of his memory. A handkerchief. Yes. The girl's handkerchief was still in the shack, stuffed inside a hollow log. It would be a pitiful object, after all this time, but it seemed important, suddenly, that the boy—her son—should have it. And the coins too; the three silver coins . . . only there were two now, weren't there, because one had paid for the fiddle . . . the boy should have those as well.

*It'll be quiet here, without him,* he thought, leaning forward on his sticks, only not too far lest the weight of his head should topple him. *I'll miss the help. I'll miss . . . him.*

'Come back,' he croaked then. 'I have more . . . much more . . . to give you.'

But it was too late. Jack had gone.

# XVII

The moon was full. It silvered the bluebells and shone upon the figure in the clearing like a big all-seeing eye. Lying back on his blanket, Jack supposed he ought to be hungry, but he wasn't. He was full, full to bursting, with plans so close to hatching that there was no room in him for anything so ordinary as food.

The ring with the blood-coloured stone in it was on a leather string around his neck. He touched it thoughtfully, and smiled up at the moon. He was imagining the future—his and Janet's—stretching, now, to the end of their lives and beyond.

For there was a beyond, he was certain of that. An eternity, waiting to happen. Not because the Old Man—*that lying hound*—had ever told him it was so. He just knew. He'd been born knowing. Heaven was somewhere, and Hell was somewhere, as surely as Janet Huckle's house was just beyond the trees. And didn't he, Jack the Lad, have as much right as anyone else to a happy-ever-afterlife?

He just had to behave himself, that was all. Control his rages. Ignore the bad thoughts. Avoid killing anyone, if he could. He might have murdered the Old Man earlier, but he hadn't, had he? He might have gone back to the monastery and stamped all over that fragment, Thomas Day, but he hadn't done that either.

*Wherever it is my bad thoughts come from*, he thought, holding tighter to his inheritance. *I am not beyond redemption.*

## Yes you are.

*No I'm not.*
He blinked at the moon. Its beams were gentle.
*Friends?* he asked it
*I'm wary,* the moon seemed to answer him back. You little whelp.

When he woke it was dawn; the wood alive with birdsong, his blanket drenched with dew. ***When will she be here?*** he fretted. Before noon, they had agreed, but noon seemed forever away. Could he wait that long? Did he have any choice?

Needing some distraction, he seized his fiddle and leapt with it onto a tree stump. It was the same stump Janet had danced on, just a few hours before. Knowing this thrilled Jack, and the tune that he played, as he tapped his boots where her small feet had been, rivalled the birdsong for sweetness.

Beyond the trees, and along the lane, in the house with gardens back and front, Annie Huckle whimpered in her sleep.

* * *

The sun rose high above the wood. Jack's stomach growled. He began to pace, for the umpteenth time, the clearing's perimeter. All morning, he had been mindful of the bluebells, taking care not to crush too many of them as he prowled, and sat, and then prowled some more. Janet's goodness, he had told himself, was already rubbing off.

Now, though, with the morning slipping into afternoon, he didn't care what he crushed. Sam Huckle should have started work by now, chopping down more trees. And Janet . . . Janet should have been right there in the clearing . . . in his arms . . . in a swoon.

## She's not coming.

*Shut up.*

## Forget her. Get away from this place . . . this back of beyond, this goat-nibbled stretch of nowhere. A boy like you could have any girl in England. Break some hearts. Stir up trouble. It's time.

*Quiet!*

He felt a panic rising in him, as the bad thoughts niggled and teased. How insistent they had become. Nastier, too. They would, he feared, drive him quite insane without his good Ja to make them go. Twelve long years he had waited for her. He would wait no more.

# XVIII

The Huckles' goose watched, beady-eyed, as Jack approached the gate. Finding it locked, Jack kicked its lowest bar. The goose hissed. Twelve-year-old Dorigan, hearing both the kick and the hiss, looked up from her seat on the doorstep. Through a dazzle of sunbeams, and vague impressions, she made out the shape of a person at the shape of the gate, and though she couldn't see the person's face, she knew that it was Him.

'Father!' she tried to call, as Jack began climbing the gate, but the word came out too faint to be heard. The goose though . . . the goose was honking for King and country as it ran, with outspread wings, at the climbing, trespassing, shape.

Had there been a goose here when he was little? Jack wondered. He didn't think there had, and found that he resented even this small change in his Ja's life.

'Call it off,' he commanded. 'And fetch your sister.' He had seen Dorigan Huckle, keeping vigil on the step, and had no doubt whatsoever that she had seen him, in her own cock-eyed way.

The goose was jabbing at his boots.

*Kill it.*

*Don't be daft.*

*Alter it, then. It's just another bird.*

*What?*

Defeated, Jack jumped back into the lane. Snapping that bird's neck would have wasted only one more moment of this already half-wasted day, but he couldn't afford to rile Sam Huckle; not before he and Ja were properly reunited and deciding how to live.

How to live ... It could have done with some thought; a bit of forward planning. But Jack the Lad, intoxicated by the bliss of having found his Ja, had swapped his wits for moonshine. He just wanted— needed—to see Janet again. The rest, he believed, would follow as naturally, and as easily, as day follows night.

'Father!' Dorigan called again, louder this time. But Sam Huckle, alerted by the goose's clamour, had already reached her side. 'It's all right, child,' he said, placing a steadying hand on her shoulder. 'Go in now, and latch the door. Wait in the bedchamber with your mother and sister. And Dorrie? Don't be scared.'

Jack watched the nuisance-sister step into the house and scowled to see the door closing behind her, with Janet the wrong side of it still. But Sam Huckle—at least, he assumed it was Sam Huckle—was walking towards him; not beaming a welcome, but not brandishing an axe, either, and so he rearranged his scowl into something more respectful and leaned over the locked gate.

'Sir,' he said, all smiles. 'I'm Jack. The boy you took, newborn, to be a companion for your daughter. The boy who . . .'

'I know who you are,' Sam interrupted, quietly.

'You do? Well then . . . I wish, if you please, to see Janet.'

Sam Huckle took a moment to shape his reply. 'Send him packing,' Annie had commanded, her voice on the edge of hysteria. 'No banter, no pleasantries. Just make him leave.' But maybe . . . just maybe . . . Annie was seeing things slant-wise, as she was sometimes prone to do, and the lad deserved a chance.

Handsome and wild were Sam's first impressions as he took Jack's measure. Extremely handsome, in fact, which was hardly a crime, but, with the wildness thrown in, might not bode well for a girl as naive and as trusting as his Jannie.

'Hold your horses, young man,' Sam said. 'And tell me: what business do you have with my daughter, that makes you speak with such urgency and cling to my gate as if a flood might tear you away from here, and wash you clear into the lake?'

112

Jack glanced down at his hands, white-knuckled from gripping the gate. Then he looked up at Sam Huckle.

'If I seem impatient, sir,' he said, 'it is because I am. Janet and I . . . we have a lot of catching up to do.'

Sam nodded. A good answer he thought; a *clever* answer. Not the truth though. No, the truth lay in the over-eager way this boy was still clutching the gate. It was burning in his eyes and darkening his face. It was radiating from him like heat from a prodded coal.

*Too passionate,* Sam concluded. *Too handsome, too wild, and too passionate, by far. Dear Jannie . . . he is too fiery for her. All that she is would be consumed by him, whether he intended it or not. Annie is right. We must send him away for a second time. Gently though. There is still no call to be cruel.*

'Tell me, Jack,' he said, gambling on the shabbiness of the boy's clothes, and the ill-fed hollows of his beautiful face. 'What are your prospects?'

'What?'

'Your prospects, boy. Your worth and standing in this world. For if you intend to court my daughter—and do not contradict me, for I see, full well, that you do—I must know that you have the means, as well as the will, to proceed. It is what any father would ask, so pray be not offended.'

Jack swallowed, hard, and his face fell as he considered his prospects and found them less than glorious.

*I am being cruel after all*, Sam realized. *But it is surely for the best.*

'Are the goats earning you a passable living?' he pressed on. 'Enough to keep a wife—children perhaps—in good comfort? With food in their bellies, and a sound roof above their heads?'

Jack blinked. He pictured the shack... what passed for its roof... spare plates cut from the end of a log... He would die of shame before taking his Ja to live there, or anywhere remotely like it. 'It was never my intention,' he said, quickly, 'to remain a humble goatherd.'

Sam nodded. 'I see. So what trade are you following now?'

Jack blinked again and cleared his throat. 'I am at a crossroads, sir,' he answered. 'The world, if you like, is my oyster.'

*Those eyes*, Sam noted, *are ... unfathomable.*

'I see,' he said. 'And I do believe that you will prosper, by and by. One day, Master Jack, you will have plenty to offer a girl like my Janet. But that day, you have to admit, is not this one.'

It was Jack's turn to nod. Earlier, he would have knocked a whole army down for standing in his way, and torn this gate clean off its fixings in order to reach his Ja. But Sam Huckle had spoken sense. Janet had lived comfortably, and well, here in this house with gardens front and back. To have imagined her leaving it, for love alone, had been hasty of him, and wrong.

*My Ja deserves the best, and I am going to get it for her. A garden front and back? My Ja will have meadows and orchards to call her very own, and a house ten times the size of this one. She will have jewels to loop around her neck and a maid to brush the tangles from her hair. These things I will get for her, within twelve months and a day. This I swear.*

**London, boy. Go to London town. You can stir a few things up there and earn a fortune into the bargain. It's time.**

*All right. Shut up.*

'Your advice is sound,' he told Sam Huckle. 'I will go from here—now, straightaway—in order to better myself. And be sure, sir, that when I return it will be as a person of high standing, with wealth enough to astonish you, and keep your daughter in splendour for the rest of her days.'

'That's the spirit,' said Sam. 'Good luck to you.' He moved to clap a friendly hand on Jack's shoulder, pleased with the boy, and with himself, for having kept things nice and civil.

'Wait,' Jack said, warding him off. 'I would speak with Janet, before I leave.'

'Ah. I'm afraid that might not . . .'

'I would speak with her, sir, or make this

spot, outside your gate, my home for the foreseeable future.'

Sam sighed.

'Listen, Jack,' he said. 'My wife, Annie—you remember Annie?—is the protective kind. Over-protective, some might say. When Jannie told us she had met with you, and had another tryst today, my Annie supposed all sorts. She leapt like a cat, from one supposing to another, none of them fair to you.'

'But . . .'

'No buts. And take it not to heart. Only be guided in this by me: go better yourself, as you intend, for in doing so you will prove yourself to Annie as well as to me, and all will be sweetly resolved.'

*Oh, break his neck and have done. Storm the house and ravish the daughter, if that is to be your pleasure. Then clobber the goose on the way out, and have it for your dinner.*

*Stop!*

Looking over Sam's shoulder, Jack gazed, with longing, on the Huckles' house. She was in there. His Ja. She was so, so close.

'Tell me,' he said to Sam Huckle. 'When my . . . when Janet told you of our tryst today, was she . . . did

116

she seem . . . eager to keep it? Would she have come to me if you had allowed it, do you think?'

He sounded so anxious, and so completely without guile, that Sam was touched. He answered truthfully: 'She is a young girl, Jack, with a young girl's dreams and fancies. And you are as comely a youth as ever was seen around these parts. So yes, she would have come.'

Jack nodded, satisfied.

'Then take her this,' he said. The ring with the blood-coloured stone in it flashed as Jack lifted it over his neck, slipped it from its string and held it out, over the gate.

'Now, Jack . . .'

'Give . . . Janet . . . this ring. And tell her I will return to her before next spring becomes the summer. I need your word on it, sir, before I leave.'

'Very well,' Sam said, taking the ring. 'You have it.'

'On your younger daughter's life?'

'Come now, there is no need . . .'

'On your younger daughter's life, sir. The matter is that heavy.'

Sam closed his eyes, disturbed by how full, suddenly, of fright and misgivings he had become.

'Very well,' he said again, hoping that this would do; that he wouldn't have to swear the thing, word for word, out loud.

'Say it,' Jack insisted. 'Say: "I swear on my younger daughter's life that I will deliver your ring, and your message, to Janet."'

'I swear on my younger daughter's life that I will deliver your ring, and your message, to Janet.'

'Good. I thank you.'

And with a final burning glance at the Huckles' closed door, Jack turned and walked away. He had no idea where London was, or how long it would take him to get there. But get there he would and then . . . ah, then . . . the future, his and Janet's, would be his for the crafting.

# XIX

Annie Huckle stared, appalled, at the ring with the blood-coloured stone. 'Whatever possessed you to accept it, husband?' she raged. 'What, in the name of all that is sacred, were you thinking?'

'Hush!' Sam rested his elbows on the family table and raked his fingers through his hair. 'She'll hear you.'

'Tsssk . . .' Annie waved a hand towards the back wall, beyond which both of their daughters were running round and round the old stone bench, laughing as they went; oblivious to whatever was happening, or being said, indoors.

'I gave him my word that she would have it,' Sam pleaded. 'My word, Annie. I can't break that.'

The ring lay between them on the table. How Annie wished she could squash it, like a currant, or a fly.

'A man's word,' she told her husband, 'counts for nothing—*nothing*, do you hear?—if it was pressed from him, like juice from a pounded plum. That boy got to you, Sam Huckle. He wore you down, addled your wits, and made you say what he wanted to hear. So you just forget about that word of yours, and we'll speak no more about it.'

She swiped up the ring, between finger and thumb, and knotted it in a corner of her apron. Later she would hide it, in a crevice in the garden wall. Throwing it into the lake would have pleased her better, but she was wise enough to know that putting someone else's love token where it could never be found was dangerous—would rebound on her, for sure.

At supper, Janet timidly enquired what had passed between her father and the boy, Jack, down at the garden gate.

Annie spoke up, before Sam could open his mouth: 'Young Master Jack has gone away,' she said, 'to make a new life for himself. He just wanted to tell us all goodbye before . . .'

'To tell *you* goodbye, Jannie,' Sam interrupted. 'To tell you goodbye, especially.'

'Me?' Janet's face pinkened.

Annie turned to glare at her husband. *You fool*, she thought. Sam paid her no mind. His eyes were on his younger daughter as she felt, with her spoon, for the food on her plate, and he was praying, silently: *Lord keep this child safe. Although I broke my word today, please keep her safe from harm.*

'Will it trouble you, not to see him again?' he asked his older girl.

Janet pondered the question. *He was handsome*, she thought. *But perhaps a little strange.* 'No, father,' she answered, honestly. 'Not really.'

Sam heard his wife sigh with relief. He, too, felt immediately better. Concealing the ring, and Jack's intentions, had, after all, been the right thing to do. His Jannie was not smitten, and they could let the matter lie. Tired, now, he set down his spoon.

'I have been thinking,' he told his family, 'of hiring an apprentice. I grow no younger, and the work I do is hard.'

'Good idea,' said Annie. 'Go to the monastery, husband. The monks are bound to know of a youth hereabouts who will be glad of such a position.'

'I will, my dear,' Sam agreed. 'Just as soon as I have the time.'

'Tomorrow,' Annie told him. 'You'll go tomorrow, husband, while there are monks, still, to be found around these parts. And, mind me Sam Huckle, it's a respectable youth we want; an apprentice of even temper and a God-fearing disposition. Do you hear me?'

'I hear you, Annie,' said Sam, with a rueful smile. 'I hear you . . .'

*You and I, my Ja, will never make our life in London, for it is Hell on earth. Too many people fill its space, clogging the streets, tumbling from doorways, vying each with the other to ply a trade or beg a coin or find pleasure in ways that I would block your ears with beeswax rather than have you hear about.*

*I play the fiddle in a tavern close by the River Thames. I play until the bow feels like part of my own arm and the fiddle like a heart, being flayed. I play for sorrow and for joy; to make men dance and weep in turn. They come from miles around, so I'm told, to hear what I can play, and I find I am much liked.*

*The keeper of the tavern feeds me pottage and bones and lets me sleep beside his hearth, with a dog's flank for a pillow. He believes that I will stay, but I will not. I bide my time. I watch the people, watching me, and wait to catch the eye of one with the means, and the fancy, to improve my situation.*

*I will know that person in a trice and will play him (or her—it might be a her) like a fish upon a hook. I will do it for us; for our future, and I will do it well.*

*The heat of summer is wretched here. The river heaves and stinks. Sickness is rife. In the evenings a kind of madness descends upon the people—a chronic desire for merriment. 'Play faster, fiddler!' they call to me, thumping the tables with their tankards and their fists.*

*The women are all bawds. They mill around the tavern in their petticoats, inciting the men to rude talk and idiocy. They tried to gain favour with me at first but understand, now, that I will* not be tempted; that I have pledged myself to you, body, heart and soul.

Bad thoughts hammer at my resolve. *Go on,* they urge. *Take pleasure while you can. Look at that one, she's almost pretty*. I play the fiddle faster . . . louder . . . to drown the bad thoughts out, and the people stamp and roar, delighted.

Fortune smiled on us tonight, Ja! It beamed from ear to ear, in fact! And I only wish that I could tell you; that I could swing you in my arms, for joy, and speak my extraordinary news, rather than keep it turning in my head where only I can know it.

I was playing idly, without much strain or effort, when a party of merrymakers fell in from the street. Straightaway I sensed change in the air: a tremor of excitement, as welcome as a breeze.

And so I watched, over my fiddle, as benches were pulled, and ale fetched, and the women all went to one man, the way that insects are drawn to the light of a splendid candle.

'Who's that?' I enquired of the first almost-sober cove to pass me by.

'Why, the Earl of Surrey,' came the reply. 'Come down river, from the King's court, for a change of pace and scene. Play faster, Master Jack, for he is fond of tavern songs.'

*I thought of you, my Ja. Of the way you
danced in the woods, with sunbeams in your hair.
Of the way you blushed, pink as a rose, when I
called you the sweetest thing. 'Might we see you
again?' you asked.*

*To see you again . . . oh, to see you again . . . I
made the fiddle sigh. I made it cry, with longing.
Then I pictured the ring—my ring—on your
finger. Saw you waiting at your father's gate,
willing your Ja to return, sooner rather than later.
And the bow in my hand grew lively, and my
feet began to stamp as I saw myself returned to
you, running down the lane.*

*The Earl of Surrey is a tall slab of a man;
battle-scarred and loud. He was carousing
with the women, his talk as foul as theirs, but
my music cut through all of that and when
he looked me in the eye I saw the poet in
him . . . and the lover . . . and the frightened
little boy.*

***He's the one,*** *I thought, and it was the
best—the most welcome—thought, Ja, that did
ever fall into my head.*

*'You play well,' the great man said to me,
when I allowed myself a lull. I bowed low and
thanked him. He continued to look at me,
as if the answer to an important question lay
somewhere on my person.*

*Take me to court, I willed him. Take. Me. To.*

*Play. For. The. King. I willed it so hard that it seemed my skull might crack.*

*'How do you fancy playing at court?' he said.*

*'It would be an honour, sir,' I answered, 'beyond my wildest imaginings.'*

*'Hmm . . .' He pondered awhile. I looked at the floor, and waited. 'The Queen—my young cousin—might find your music pleasing,' he said at last. 'But . . .' he wagged a warning finger at me, 'should His Majesty not approve, you'll be booted out, like a yowling hound. You'll be out before you can blink, swallow, or say adieu to the pretty ladies.'*

*I bowed again, hiding a smile. And the chuckle that rumbled between my two ears was both wicked and victorious. Good boy, I heard myself think. Well played.*

*Finding myself at court, Ja, has fair dazzled all my senses. The beauty of it! The grandeur! Don't laugh, but it has given me a bit of a headache— there is so much to take in; so much I need to learn.*

*It was late last night, when I jumped into a barge and was conveyed along the river to the steps of Whitehall Palace. They were such ordinary looking steps, Ja—slippery wooden things, slopped over by the water—that I held back, thinking myself deceived. It made Lord*

125

Surrey chortle, to see me so perplexed. 'Should we have brought you to the Privy Steps, to tread where princes tread?' he teased. 'With banners unfurled, and a fanfare of trumpets to welcome you back on dry land?'

He hurried me, then, through moonlit grounds, and candlelit passageways into a kitchen ten times the size, I swear, of your father's house, where half a dozen serving folk were eating a midnight feast. And there he left me, with instructions to drink little and sleep well, for tomorrow could make or break me.

Those servants gave me bread and meat, and a place among them at their table. They made me welcome, I suppose, but not in a manner that pleased me. Indeed, I could have been a two-headed cat, or a mouse that can count to twenty—a novelty, anyway, plucked from the streets for the amusement of higher beings.

'You pretty, pretty boy,' one of the women sighed, touching my face as if it were a holy relic. 'Never mind how you do make that fiddle sing. Just to look upon you tomorrow night, across the heads of old men, will surely please Queen Katherine.'

The others laughed muckily, all except one: a young man whose curled lip told me, straight off, that he considers himself a cut above his fellows.

'Come, Thomas Culpeper,' his neighbour did

*say, nudging him in the ribs. 'Get down from*
*your tall horse, and crack us a proper smile.'*

*Thomas Culpeper bared his teeth, in a poor*
*excuse for a grin. Then: 'I give you all good*
*night,' he said, and stood to take his leave.*

## Watch him.

*The thought drummed between my ears*
*before Master Culpeper was out of the door.*

## It is in our—your—best interests, my sweet, to watch him like a hawk.

*I ate well, but drank little, as My Lord Surrey*
*had advised. And I woke, a short while ago, on a*
*good, clean pallet in a chamber that, though set*
*aside for servants, does suit me very well.*

*Through a window, set high, I can see that dawn*
*is breaking. I pray that this day will be lucky for us.*
*That I will acquit myself well, with my playing, and*
*that King Henry and Queen Katherine (The King*
*and Queen of England, Ja! How astonishing is that?)*
*will think me a genius, Heaven-sent.*

*It is time—time for me to play. And I wish, Ja,*
*with all my heart, that you were here to give*
*me courage. Courage and a kiss. What wouldn't*
*I give for your kiss? I swear, my lips grow*

parched for the want of it. But enough. I must concentrate.

The feast has been eaten (they brought in a swan Ja—a whole swan!—roasted and swimming in wine) and the dancing has begun.

The mood, so far, has been sedate; the men and the women stepping together, then stepping apart, to the mewling of recorders and the watery strains of a lute. This worries me. Do they prefer, then, to be dull, here at court? If so they will like me not.

My fingers feel quite useless. Sluggish. Unprepared. I will them to buck up. I remind myself that the Queen is young—seventeen, so I've been told—and that she loves to dance. Surely to goodness she, at least, will welcome a merrier pace? That's her, in red, and she is looking straight up at me. Groups of noblemen, huddled like ravens, are looking at me too; as are all the ladies who, until now, have been flitting from man to man, like the bawds in the tavern only better dressed. The King sits on his throne: a glittering toad, his bad leg thrust out at an angle. He is looking at me hardest of all.

I cannot lie, Ja, I am trembling all over now, like a winter leaf. The importance of this moment, and all that rests upon it, weighs so heavily on me that I cannot move at all. The fiddle beneath my chin might as well be made of lead, so hefty and tuneless does it feel. The bow

trails, useless, from my fingers. In a moment, I
might drop it.

But: **Ruin this,** I think, **and you'll
wish you had never been born.** I
close my eyes. I take a gulp of air that tastes of
swan. I imagine you, hovering bright and good at
my shoulder.

I raise my bow and begin to play.

The tune is full of mischief. It bounces off
vast tapestries and twirls around the pillars. Up
to the beams it flies, as merry as you like, then
down . . . down . . . to frisk a pretty pattern on
the floor. It tells of blue skies, bisected by larks,
and of girls hop-skipping round May poles. It
sings of dew falling, and sap rising, and of young
men, drunk on love and cider, stumbling into
ditches.

Queen Katherine is . . . well . . . laughing. I
have my eyes downcast but I know it is her. She
has an irritating laugh, high-pitched and silly.
It is putting my teeth on edge. It is making me
sweat. Does she mock me? Does she . . . dare?
Now all her ladies are doing it. Tee-heeing in
unison. Squealing like tickled pigs. And I must
focus . . . focus . . . on the fiddle, and on you. For
I cannot . . . will not . . . falter.

**Play on, boy. Play on. The stakes
are high. Play on.**

*The bad voice is calm, and steadies me. Right now, it is my friend.*

*I dare to look up—one swift glance, as the sweat flies from my hair and my right arm cramps, from the playing—and it's all right! It's all right, Ja—the Queen . . . she's dancing! Look, there she goes, linking the arm of first one courtier . . . then another . . . romping the whole length of the hall. Her red skirts swirl, her long hair swings. She has no idea, really, how to dance to the tune I am fiddling, but no matter. Her giggles do not mock me. She is having a wonderful time.*

*Behind my back, established court musicians glare at me (I know, I can sense it). They are willing my fingers to slip, my notes to ring false, and my nerve to fail entirely. And you know what, Ja? They are going to be disappointed.*

*I risk a quick glance at the King. His eyes are on his Queen. He is drinking her in, as she dances, and he, too, is laughing. It amuses him, I realize, to watch his young wife lift her jewel-encrusted skirts to go gallumping round the hall, like a low-born village lass. More than that—it excites him.*

*I look away, lest my gaze should be felt by His Royal Fatness, and taken for impertinence. Bending to the finish of my tune, I spy Thomas Culpeper leaning against a pillar. He, like the King, has eyes only for Queen Katherine. He is*

*watching her intently, the way a stoat will watch
a vole. A smirk lifts a corner of his mouth.*

*I end my performance with a flourish. My
heart is bumping as I bow to the King, then to
the Queen, then to everyone else. The Earl of
Surrey has just tipped me the smallest of nods. It
is a sign—a very sure sign—of approval.*

*Everything, Ja, is going our way. I am so deep in
favour with the King, in fact, that it is whispered
among the servants that he can no longer fall
asleep unless I stand beside his bed, playing
cradle songs, as if to a fretful child.*

*Such talk is not far wrong. King Henry
retires late, worn out by leg-pain, and matters of
State. He is attended first by Thomas Culpeper,
who must bathe, and then bind, the putrid
ulcer on the royal leg. My job, by comparison, is
a delight.*

*Thomas Culpeper is always in a rush to be
wherever it is he goes after bidding the King
goodnight. Perhaps he is merely glad to be
done with the sight and stench of that ulcer,
but I believe there is more to it. There is a
spring to his step and mischief in his eyes when
we cross paths, as we usually do, outside His
Majesty's chamber.*

*'Have fun,' he says to me—always the same
two words, followed by a snigger; the implication*

being that it is he, not I, who is about to have some fun, and that the very thought of it makes him feel about ten yards tall, with a crown of his own on his head.

## Watch him.

It is a tryst with some girl, I expect, that gives Culpeper his swagger. But it's his business, not mine, so why must I watch him? I push such thoughts away. I have other fish to fry.

The King lies on a high bed hung all about with cloths of scarlet and gold. I must read his mood, the way a learned man might read a book, and play music to suit it, precisely.

This is hard work, Ja, and I do dread the arrival of bad thoughts at this time of the day. Thankfully, they have not come. Indeed, I have perfected the art of entering His Majesty's chamber with my mind empty and my face blank, so that nothing of myself—of who, or what I am—will detract from the sound of my playing.

The King likes my stillness. He likes it a lot. And these past few nights, with his leg a little better, and his mood a little lighter, he has been asking me all manner of questions. Where am I from? What name do I go by? What brought me to London?

Tonight, I told him about you. 'Ah,' he said, with the flick of a smile. 'So the fiddler, like his

King, has a rose without a thorn. Does she wait for you?'

For certain, Majesty, I told him, for we are pledged.

He grunted then, already bored. 'Play,' he commanded and then, a while later: 'Leave.'

King Henry is a fickle man. I left as quietly as I'd arrived, but oh, my Ja, how good it felt to say your name and hear it echo in that magnificent room, as true as any note of music.

My rose without a thorn.

That's you. Yes, that's you, exactly.

The longer I am at court, Ja, the less I admire its workings. The King, I have concluded, is envied more than loved. And feared, too, for the pendulum-swing of his moods. It is said he will have a condemned man beheaded, or pardoned and set free, depending on the weather and how well he enjoyed his breakfast.

The men I see regularly milling around strike me as cunning types. My Lord Surrey calls them flatterers and deceivers, all out for what they can get. The Howards and the Seymours spat like cats on a wall, each faction waiting, I suspect, for an excuse to topple the other from the King's most gracious favour.

Not long ago, Ja, I was mocked for being ill-versed in the true ways of this world. Now my head could split, so ripe is it with all I have come to know and understand.

At night, their tongues loosened by wine, titled men gather in twos and threes, at the very edge of the hall, to swap tales and information. I listen, when I can. If they are aware of my shadow, bending their way, it troubles them not. After all, I am only the fiddle player.

**Keep listening, boy,** croons the voice in my head, **until something smacks of treason.**

The servants, too, have loose tongues, but while high-ranking men do talk on heavy matters—wealth, warfare and the flushing out of heretics—these lower-born types are more interested in who is lying with who at night, and whether it be for love or just the pleasuring of their parts.

Joan Bulmer, one of the Queen's ladies, could tell me things (or so she claims) that would make my hair curl and my jaw drop as if broken. This Joan would lie with me in a twinkling, she has as good as said so. **Go on,** the bad voice urges. **Live a little, milksop.** But I would sooner be sliced where it really hurts, like a prized singing boy, than lie with any girl in this life, apart from you.

\* \* \*

The bad voice grows tiresome, and harder to ignore. *Go to Joan,* it insists. *Her pillow talk could serve us well—and make you rich beyond your wildest dreams.* It slithers into my head, that voice, the moment I'm awake. It distracts me while I'm playing—even when I'm playing for the King, late at night—and bellows while I eat, or drink, so loud I almost choke. *Go to Joan. Go!*

Last night I dreamt that someone had stolen my fiddle. I was in the woods—the bluebell woods close by your father's house—and could hear my fiddle playing, through the trees. I ran, Ja, towards the sound, and as I ran strange flowers grew to block my way; their petals and leaves such violent shades of orange and red that they did seem to lick at me, like flames. 'Give me back what is mine!' I hollered into this blaze. Then a bony finger did tap my shoulder and I whirled round to find a man before me—a man cloaked and hooded, with a beard such as a goat might sport and eyes with blood in the whites.

'I know you,' I cried out. 'I've watched for you at the market. You used to own the fiddle, but it's mine now, and I want it back. Can you get it for me?'

He opened his mouth. I saw smoke in there. *Go to Joan,* he said.

\* \* \*

135

I went, Ja. I went to Joan. She leaves today, on
a progress to the north with Queen Katherine,
the King and a retinue that will stretch for
several miles (I had thought to be a part of
it but no—there will be musicians enough,
apparently, to entertain their majesties along
the way).

All yesterday the bad voice did harangue
me: *If you don't visit Joan tonight,
you little weasel, good fortune will
desert you, and calamity nip, for
ever, at your heels. For ever, my
sweet . . . is that a thing you care
to risk, hmmm?*

I swear, Ja, I did not touch her. Not in THAT
way. She bade me meet her after midnight in
Thomas Culpeper's chamber, for we would be
private there, she said, and as cosy as two
sparrows in a nest.

When I got there, she was lying on the bed,
her hair and her shift loose. There were tall
candles burning, and a fire lit.

I looked down at her and she smirked at me
and then raised herself up on her elbows, causing
her shift to gape the more. 'Well, Master Jack,'
she said. 'Do you like—hic—what you see?'

Ja, trust me when I tell you, I hated what I saw.
The girl was drunk. A wanton mess. But she had
knowledge of something: something I knew I might

use to our advantage if the bad voice spoke true, which I had come to believe it did.

So I reached out my longest finger, and traced with it the outline of Joan's mouth. She shivered a little, and grabbed my wrist. 'Come on,' she murmured, tugging at me. 'Lie with me, Jack. You won't . . . hic . . . regret it.'

'Nah,' I said, as if already bored. 'A quick tumble, Joan, before Culpeper returns would be—well—unpalatable to me. I like to take my time.'

Letting go my wrist, she sat up, quickly, then clutched at the quilt as if the bed did rock or spin. 'I know for a FACT,' she said in an exaggerated whisper, 'that Thomas Culpeper will not . . . hic . . . be back before dawn.'

'Will he not?'

I considered her hair—rats' tails compared to yours, Ja—and somehow knew to take a long, thick strand of it between my fingers and begin winding it, slowly, slowly round my fist. In this way I did force her up onto her feet, and then towards me, until our two faces were very close.

'I'm not sure I trust this "fact" Joannie,' I murmured into her ear. 'For how would you know?'

'Because . . .' She pressed herself against me, half-naked as she was and, yes, it felt . . .

interesting . . . but, Ja, she might as well have been a broom, with two apples slung around its stick, for all the delight I took from such intimacy with a girl who is not you.

I tightened my grip on her hair and raised my free hand to stroke her cheek. Force and sweetness . . . it confused her, yet pleased her too, for she moaned the softest moan, then made as if to kiss me on the mouth.

'Because what, Joan?' I asked, holding fast to her hair so that our lips would not meet. 'Because what?'

She closed her eyes and gave a little huff-and-sigh of frustration. I smelled spices and wine on her breath and felt the sailor-sway of her hips.

'Because . . . he ish with . . . his lady love,' she slurred. 'His turtle dove. Hish . . . hic . . . treasure.'

I let the fingers of my left hand trail all along her jawbone, down the length of her throat, to touch the soft skin below the dip of her collarbone. Then I dug my nails in. It was like playing the fiddle, Ja. It was like knowing when to speed up, and when to slow down; when to let the bow glide and when to make it jab.

'Then I'll bid thee goodnight, sweet Joan,' I said, releasing my hold on her, and stepping away. 'For I have come to know Master Culpeper. And no serving maid, however comely, would keep him long from the comfort of his own bed. Not

138

when he must rise early, these days, to tend to
His Majesty's leg.'

'Ah, but . . .' She flung herself at me,
giggling, and aiming kisses at my throat. 'It is
no . . . serving maid . . . he's pleasuring . . .' She
broke off, then, from both the kissing and the
telling, and covered her mouth with both hands.
'Oops,' she said, all muffled. 'I mushtn't say any
more . . .'

I peeled her off me. I told her I was vexed.
I said she could keep her silliness all to herself,
for I had no wish to hear whatever lie she had
concocted just to keep me with her in that room.

"Tis not silliness. Jack,' she insisted, clinging to
the back of my shirt as I made as if to go. 'And no
concoction either, for I would not lie to you.' The
thought of my leaving must have sobered her,
for there was no hiccoughing now, or slurring of
her words. I did not reply, but nor did I move any
further towards the door. I just stood very still, with
my back to her, and waited.

I had guessed, by then, Ja, what it was that she
was party to. I had worked it out. Still, I needed
to hear it said.

The knowledge, when she spoke it, soaked
into me like sunshine, for I understood its worth.

'The Queen,' she whispered to the back
of my neck. 'Thomas Culpeper does lie with
the Queen.'

139

*I did not know, at first, who to tell. I had to
think, long and hard, about that. Certainly, it was
not my place to let slip to the King of England
that his rose without a thorn was being pleasured
by his groom. No. His Majesty would have had
me thrown in the Tower for gross impudence,
whatever the truth of the matter. And, anyway,
he wasn't home. He had left for the north, as
planned, with his false Queen riding by his side
and Culpeper close behind.*

*Archbishop Cranmer, I thought,
after a while. That's who you'll tell. I
trust such thoughts now, Ja, and why not? They
are serving us well, you and I.*

*It was some time before the Archbishop came
to court, and sweet chance that I happened to
spy him as he took the air, alone, around the
chapel garden. I leapt a hedge of lavender in
my eagerness to apprehend the man, and almost
sprawled, headlong, at his feet. I had my fiddle
with me and was glad about that, thinking His
Grace might recognize me as the King's favourite
musician and accord me a little respect.*

*Respect? Hah! Respect be fried in a dirty pan
and thrown to the crows. Archbishop Cranmer
looked at me as if I needed shovelling up. He
listened, though. Oh how greedily he did listen,
to all I had to say.*

*We'll get him, too, one day,* I thought, **and watch him burn, like a stick.** The thought was faint—barely there. Still, it made me pause, in the telling of my tale. And as that pause opened out, into a silence, Thomas Cranmer did stare deep into my eyes and I . . . I became afraid.

What does he behold? I wondered. What demons might he see in me that I would prefer to keep well hidden? (From all, that is, except my Ja, who understands.) I wanted to flee. Not just over the lavender bushes, but down the River Thames, and far away from court. But that would have ruined everything.

I thought of you. I pictured your face. And, with no small effort, began, again, to talk.

Go, he told me, when I was finally done. And do not speak of this to another living soul.

I walked carefully away, sensing those holey eyes upon me; aware of the learned mind at work behind them, assessing my news. Assessing me. And although I ought to have rejoiced—silently, to myself—at the thought of a hand well played, I did nothing of the kind. Nor am I doing so now, six—almost seven—days later.

A pastry cook, here at the palace, did recently tut to hear a kitchen maid describe her wedding gown, down to the last pretty flounce, when she has yet to be looked at sideways by a lad, never mind pledged. 'Do not count your chickens, Bess, until they all be hatched,' was what he said to this giddy girl.

And so I wait, counting only the days, until whatever plan the Archbishop has laid shows signs of hatching out.

Autumn has put a chill in the air. The King's gardeners are burning leaves, the piles as high as haystacks. A mist does rise, each evening, from the river. I sense danger, Ja, seeping into this place, with the leaf-smoke and the mist. It smells, to me, of sulphur.

They took Joan Bulmer first. Then me. Then Lady Jane Rochford, who does wait upon the Queen. Then one Francis Dereham, come recently to court to be Her Majesty's personal secretary. Queen Katherine, it transpires, knew Dereham before her marriage to the King. Knew him very well indeed, by all accounts.

Joan and I were released, once we had told all that we knew. Lady Rochford and Dereham were not. I passed Joan this evening, on my way to the King's chamber. She looked thinner than I remember, and nowhere near as pleased to see me as before.

I caught her by the elbow and placed my lips against her ear. 'Did they threaten you, Joan?' I whispered. 'Did they show you the rack and those

142

screws that crush your toe bones?' She bade me
crawl away and die.

You would be relieved to know, Ja, that your
Jack the Lad acquitted himself most marvellously,
through I don't know how many hours of
questioning. So marvellously, in fact, that he was
shown only courtesy, and the occasional tight-
lipped smile.

Think not, though, that I remained
complacent throughout, for I knew (and it fair
melted my bowels to know it) that one wrong
word . . . one flicker of something in my face
that Cranmer and the others could take against,
and those questions would have taken a truly
nasty turn.

The Archbishop and his cronies might have
wondered, Ja, whether I, too, had ever dallied
with Her Majesty. For she did gaze upon me
most favourably in the great hall, and, according
to Joan Bulmer, found me devilish handsome.
They could have pinned that on me, Ja. Had it
suited their purpose to be rid of me, they could
have tortured me cruelly, and arraigned me for
treason. But they didn't.

Eventually, they took Thomas Culpeper.
Then they came for the Queen.

The King does not converse with me, these
nights. 'Play,' he commands, through gritted

teeth. Then he turns his face away, lest I see the anguish in it and dare to pity him.

Does he know that it was I who went to Cranmer? He must do. And will he reward me for it, by and by? I would be mad to ask. I dare not even think it—at least not in his presence—for it is more important now than ever that the only feelings I churn up in this powerful, dangerous man relate to the music that must, somehow, bring him rest.

And so I play. I play of the grief that follows loss, as it surely will, and let the rise and spill of the tune remind King Henry that even the sharpest of sorrows will pass. I play of ice melting, and storms passing, and of joy found, when you least expect it. I play of a clearing in a wood, where sunlight may enter; of birdsong and the thudding of an axe, with the birdsong lasting longest. Of the way a head may turn, as if pulled by a string, and a broken heart mend and leap at the sound of someone's voice.

And 'Leave,' he says, as his tears come. But he says it gently, Ja, so that I may know, without being told, that he is not vexed with me. That, on the contrary, he considers this weeping to be as necessary to his recovery as the letting of blood can be, for a fever. I must be the only person in the whole world, Ja, who can make the King of England cry, without losing His gracious favour. Or my life.

* * *

I did not attend the executions of Francis
Dereham and Thomas Culpeper. Dereham had
his innards pulled out, while he still drew breath,
and did twitch and gag to see them, so I'm told.
The severing of his head must have come as
a mercy to that man. *Milksop,* I thought
afterwards. *Why didn't you go? It was
some spectacle . . .*

Culpeper got off lightly, being merely dragged
through the crowds and beheaded. Had I been
King it would have been the other way round:
a quick death for Dereham and a slow one for
Master Culpeper, whose liaison with the Queen
was, after all, the more recent, and most heinous,
of betrayals.

But the King, so it is whispered, did hate
Dereham the most for being the first (if we can
believe it) to lie with Katherine Howard, thus
spoiling her for marriage, and a place in the
royal heart.

Culpeper's head does leer, now, from a spike near
Traitor's Gate. Queen Katherine (although I should
no longer be calling her that) would have seen it,
on her own way to The Tower. And if she didn't,
I'll wager one of her guards will have pointed it out,
just to hammer home, for the good of her soul (or,
more likely, his own amusement) the sheer folly of
her ways.

*It is bitter cold this morning, Ja. There is
frost on the cobbles and the folk who move,
and surge, to get a better view of the scaffold,
are well wrapped up. I am here with the King's
pastry cook—he of the 'don't count your
chickens' incident—and he has just passed to
me a honey crust, fresh-baked. It is very good.
Indeed, it fair melts in my mouth and I cannot
help but wonder how it must feel to know that
you have swallowed your last crumb in this world.*

*My companion is recounting some tale about
the Bishop of Rochester's cook, boiled alive in his
own pot for having peppered a soup with poison.
The Bishop survived, I'm told, but two of his
dinner guests did not. And the boiling idea was
King Henry's. A most fitting end for a poisoner, do
I not agree?*

*I have been saved the bother of replying
by the arrival of the executioner. We are close
enough, the pastry cook and I, to see the muscles
in his arms, as big and round as basins, and to
note that the blade of his axe is both sharp
and clean.*

*Now come the guards. One has Lady Rochford
by the arm, escorting her as if to dinner. The
lady looks bewildered but then her mind, so it is
said, has quite gone to the fairies, so perhaps she
thinks she really is about to dine.*

*It was Lady Roch, Ja, who did encourage*

Queen Katherine to be a lewd and naughty girl. She also kept vigil, outside Her Majesty's chamber, while Her Majesty frolicked with Culpeper. The pastry cook is hoping she will rant and rave at first sight of the axe, and make a fine show of herself. He never did like her, much.

The Queen—Katherine Howard, I should say—is mounting the scaffold unaided. At least, I must assume it is she, for this slight girl, with her hair stuffed into a cap, looks nothing like the one who did dance to my tunes at Whitehall, not so very long ago.

Is she . . . ? Yes, she is—she is speaking. She sounds like a little girl. She begs forgiveness—from the King, from God, from all of us—for her wickedness. She says she deserves to die. She is looking, not outward, but up at the sky, as if that is where she most hopes to be heard.

'God save you,' some woman calls.

*Or not, I think.*

What's this? Something untoward is happening. A scuffle and some squealing. It is Lady Roch. She is struggling to free herself from the grip of her guard; saying it's me, now, it's my turn, unhand me. She actually sounds excited, like a child with a verse to sing. 'Not yet, my lady,' her guard tells her, holding firm to her arm. 'Not yet . . .'

Katherine Howard has just said something to one of the other guards. I'm not sure I caught it, but think it was, 'Is it time?' She seems uncertain about what happens next. Or perhaps, with only moments left to live, her mind is making a blank of itself, and her body refusing to move.

Beside me, the pastry cook has broken wind. He is such a churl. Those nearest to us are tutting, or snorting with barely suppressed laughter. 'Sorry,' the pastry cook says, fanning the air as the smell of him rises. 'Sorry, all.'

Katherine Howard is being led to the block. Her feet are bare and must be cold. She moves gracefully, though, these last few steps and when she falls to her knees, it's like a curtsey.

I wonder if she will look up, wanting one last glimpse of another—any living creature— and, yes, as if reading my thoughts, she is doing exactly that. She has raised her head and is . . . well . . . looking straight at me. Am I to be cursed then? Does she deliberately look my way? But no . . . her gaze is blank. Unseeing. She is preparing herself, that's all.

And now she is bending to the block . . . laying her head down as if upon a pillow and closing her eyes. I can see that she is shivering, but that could just be from the cold. Her neck is very white.

Somewhere to my right, a woman has begun

a-weeping and I wonder, crossly, why. I want to shout at her to be quiet. To save her tears for someone, or something, else. Katherine Howard deserves to die. She's just said as much herself.

The executioner has raised the axe. His muscles bulge and it seems he might hold that pose for ever, so still is he, and so steady. And I'm marvelling Ja——I can't help it——at the way I . . . we . . . appear stuck in this moment as if for all time. As if the axe will never fall . . . the morning frost never melt . . . and Katherine Howard never do more than rest upon that block, drifting in and out of sweet and silly dreams.

'Ugh!' grunts the pastry cook, clutching at my arm.

And that still and perfect moment has ended, now, in a wave of exclamation, and the dancing of the victim's feet as her head is taken off.

The King's mood brightens, daily. He has a new groom, a new horse, and more vigour for hunting first thing and making merry into the night. There are fresh women at court. They preen and twitter for His Majesty's pleasure but, should he single one out to speak to, I cannot help but note, how many do raise a hand to their throats, as if to check their heads.

My thoughts have been babbling, like a brook full of rain.

Catholics . . . Lutherans . . . the
Howards . . . the Seymours . . .
we'll bring 'em all down, by and
by. The good . . . the bad . . . the
new and the old . . . we'll muddy
the waters, boy, and kick up a
storm. We'll put many a living
soul in jeopardy as they wonder
who or what to believe in and
whether, and how, to pray. And
oh, the fun of it . . . the merry,
merry fun . . .

I do think such nonsense, sometimes, that I
wonder at it. Shut up, I tell myself. And: where
is my reward for alerting Cranmer, and the King,
to the true and devious nature of the not-much-
lamented Queen?

Never mind that, the bad voice
snarls. For there is more to do and
I would not have you distracted.
You'll get your reward, my sweet,
but not here on earth. Think on it.

Oh tish and tosh, I think. Tish, tosh and a
tailor's token. I've had enough of this place. I
want to go home to my Ja. She'll be expecting
me. It's time. But first, I must have what I
am owed.

*It is resolved! Oh, my Ja, it is all so sweetly*
*resolved! It was Lord Surrey who brought me*
*the news. I was in the great hall, tuning up my*
*fiddle, and expecting nothing more from the rest*
*of the day than to play my tunes, as usual, and*
*then to sleep and dream of you.*

*The King and his guests were dining, still,*
*but would be dancing by and by, and wanting*
*it lively. The King steps out well enough*
*these days, on his gammy leg—out to prove, I*
*suspect, to the ladies and to himself, that he is*
*as sprightly, still, as a man of twenty, and quite*
*recovered from recent events. Still, the sight of*
*him, step-lurching up and down this hall, would*
*make a pot guffaw, so I have learned to play*
*lively, but to suit a jerky pace. In this way, Ja, I*
*have devised a whole new rhythm which will*
*doubtless be the fashion, by and by, in courts*
*all over Europe. I would call it the King's Sorry*
*Shuffle if it were safe for me to do so. But it's*
*not safe, so I don't.*

*Lord Surrey, having found me at my tuning,*
*did check the hall all round for eavesdroppers*
*(there were none). Then 'Jack,' he said to me,*
*gravely, 'I bring news, about your future.' I'll*
*admit, that got me worried, he did look and sound*
*so grim, and his next words, far from lifting up*
*my spirits, hit me like punches, well-aimed.*

'You are to leave court,' he said, as solemn as you like. 'Not straightway, but soon.'

My face fell, Ja. I felt it drop. And my heart dropped too—right to the pit of my belly. What could I possibly have done, I wondered, to displease His Majesty so? Where was I to go, and what would I do, and WHAT ABOUT MY REWARD?

I felt giddy: fit to faint like an ailing maid, for everything seemed in vain, and you lost to me for longer than I could bear to think about. Only when Lord Surrey gave a laugh like the roar of a lion did I realize that he was toying with me and that maybe . . . just maybe . . .

'Your face!' My Lord cuffed me, playfully. 'But listen . . . listen carefully now, for you have the luck of the Devil . . .'

Ja, my reward is beyond generous. I am to be given some land, and a house to go with it. And not just a bit of old pasture, either, or a dwelling so mean that a gust of wind could flatten it. No. I am to have one of the monasteries that belong, now, to the King. The smallest of the lot, according to Lord Surrey—too meanly proportioned to go to a man of any account, but more, much more, than a lad of my age and low birth could ever hope to gain through his own poor endeavours.

'It's ramshackle,' My Lord informed me, 'and in some godforsaken backwater. But there's

152

enough land, all around, to provide a steady income, if you manage it well. And it has pleased the King to have the place made habitable, and furnished to what he trusts will be your liking. It should all be finished by Easter. Are you glad?'

I said I was. I said I was fit to expire from gladness and that my gratitude knew no bounds. I said I might have to sit down and . . .

'All right,' he interrupted, crossly. 'That's enough. I will convey your thanks to His Majesty, for you will play no more in his chamber, only here, for the dancing, until the day comes for you to leave. Do you understand?'

I didn't. But I do now, for I have given the matter much thought. Think on it, Ja: of course the King wants rid of me. For fond though His Lurchiness is of my playing, and grateful, too, for its comfort, I am bound to remind him—how could I not? —of his time with the former Queen.

Henry could have just kicked me out, Ja. He could have banished me from court with no more than my fiddle, and the clothes I arrived in. (And, even then, he might have kept the fiddle.) But I like to think, I really do, that he has not forgotten all I said to him, once, about you. And that, having discovered his own rose to be thick, after all, with thorns, he does wish me better luck, and a life of pleasure and ease, with my own blameless girl.

'One more thing,' Lord Surrey added, before turning his back on me, 'You cannot be a man of means without a family name. You don't have one do you? No, His Majesty thought not, and it has amused him to grant you one.'

On first hearing, Ja, my given name sounds odd. But I'll get used to it and so, I trust, will you, as you will share it soon. It is the name given by learned men to a pattern of stars that fling light across the darkest sky.

Orion.

I am Jack Orion. And I will return to you, as I promised I would, before the spring is out. My heart is light. My thoughts are sweet. I am so very happy.

# XX

The gossip, Kate Bundy, had heard the rumour from her husband, who had heard it in the tavern from the man whose son always kept his ears well-pricked and had heard it while delivering a cartload of manure to the old monastery garden, for the feeding, and growing, of some thousand scarlet roses.

''Tis said the new owner be little more than a boy,' Kate told the honey-seller at the market. 'Imagine? He'll be rattling around that great big house like a knuckle bone in a crypt. And crying for his mammy, too, I do expect, when the shadow of the Holy Cross begins to form across his table, or the tolling of a bell he can neither see nor find, does keep him awake at night.'

The honey-seller let flick at a fly with half a horse's tail tied to a stick. No one wanted honeycomb stuck all over with creepy crawlies, and this spring had been so wretched hot that the flies had come out early, to make a nuisance of themselves. 'Is the old monastery truly haunted, then, Kate?' she asked. 'For it has been so knocked about and altered that surely no monk, dead or alive, would know it now?'

Kate Bundy sucked on her teeth and shrugged. 'The stonemason has said it be so,' she declared. 'For he stayed overnight in the place while putting it to rights, and swears to have seen the shadow of the cross and heard snatches of mass being sung.'

'So how soon will our young master be in residence?'

Again, Kate shrugged. She had no idea. Nor could she tell the honey-seller why roses were being planted, in such glorious profusion, where once the monks raised cabbages and rows of hanging beans.

'He could arrive any day,' she said. 'For Sam Huckle has finished the bed. Carved all over, he says it is, with beasties, and birds and vines. And up on a dais, if you please, with embroidered curtains sent from Italy and a mattress so soft and wide you would think yourself in Paradise, asleep on a squishy cloud.'

The honey-seller licked her lips, as if the image could be tasted. 'Such magnificence,' she sighed, 'and all for some slip of a lad.'

'A *wealthy* slip of a lad,' Kate reminded her. 'An *eligible* slip of a lad too, I do suppose, for I've not heard tell of a wife. My youngest lass has charms enough, I'm hoping, to catch his eye 'ere long.'

'Hah!' The honey-seller swished, so hard, at a bluebottle, that the cart tipped and almost fell. 'Yes,' she added, halting the slow slide of her honeycombs, with both her sticky hands. 'Your Alice has charms a-plenty—enough to catch a dead man's eye and make it twinkle like a star. And this fine young gent will be glad of a buxom lass to cling to, I'll wager, when them long-dead monks do start their midnight chantings . . .'

'I see it plainly, neighbour. What mirth!' Kate slapped her own thigh and laughed, long and loud. The foot that had gone peculiar, almost a year ago, and in this very place, felt weighty all of a sudden. She had to stamp it, in the dirt, to stop it going numb.

# XXI

'He wants what?' Sam Huckle frowned at the stonemason, then turned to consider what he'd taken to be a fully-finished building (manor ... great house ... he knew what others called it but to him it was just a building, and a vulgar one at that).

'Initials,' the mason repeated. 'There look, above the door. Two "J"s, intertwined.'

Sam sighed and scratched his head. 'It's too late to be adding such fripperies,' he grumbled. 'He'll be here any day, won't he? And this'll be some job—assuming, that is, he wants the letters tall and the carving fine.'

'Sorry,' the mason said. 'I've only just had word. Share the task with whatsisname—your apprentice—why don't you, for his work is fine enough.'

'Hmm,' Sam squinted at the space above the grand oak door, measuring it with his eye, imagining the two 'J's, like a couple of snakes, embracing.

'Why wooden letters?' he asked. 'Why not stone?'

'Search me,' the mason said. 'I'm just passing on the details. Will you do it?'

'All right,' Sam agreed. 'I'll do it.'

'Good man. One other thing I've heard: the lad be recently wed—or is soon to be wed, I forget which. Perchance he has only just thought this up, as a surprise for his new bride? A pretty slip from court she'll be, I expect. A Jane or a Julia.'

'No doubt,' Sam said, although a chill had settled on him. 'Tell me.' he said to the mason, 'what is the name—the family name—of this boy so greatly favoured by the King?'

The mason had to think about that. He could chisel any name to perfection, on most types of stone, but remembering them . . . ah, that was another matter. Same with faces, unless they belonged to angels and had been exquisitely sculpted from marble, or granite, or ice. He just wasn't all that interested in other human beings. Never had been. 'Begins with an "O",' he said, after a few moments' thought. 'O'Reilly . . . O'Ryan . . . something like that. Irish, anyway, by the sound of him.'

Relief made Sam Huckle generous. 'We will do a good job of the letters,' he promised. 'But must be finished and away by Friday noon as we, too, have a wedding planned.'

'Of course,' the mason answered, quickly. 'I hadn't forgotten that.'

159

# XXII

There were no servants waiting to greet the new master of Orion House, for they had yet to be taken on. And the coachman who had driven Jack from London was told to stop at the tavern, and rest there overnight, before going back the way he had come.

'I can walk from here,' Jack said, leaping down from his seat. 'Just pass me my fiddle, will you.'

The coachman stared, perplexed. 'But what about your boxes, sir?' he wondered. 'Won't you be wanting your things?'

Jack looked up at the boxes, all carefully stacked and tied on.

Things.

Did he want his things? His Venetian goblets of blood-red glass . . . his many spoons for soups, and jellies . . . his compass nestled, like a silver egg, in a container enamelled with stars? His beeswax candles . . . his sable cloak . . . his horse whip and his slippers? The quill pen and the inks, for making his mark as he knew, now, how to do? The chess set, with the ivory pieces, which he knew, now, how to play?

'Have them kept here,' he told the coachman. 'I'll send for them by and by.' And, with his fiddle on his back and a big smile on his face, he turned and strode away.

*Crazed*, thought the coachman. *As mad as a March hare.*

'I know that boy!'

The coachman peered down to see the keeper of the tavern—stout, red-faced—pointing, and panting, and looking as stunned as a man can look without having suffered a sharp blow to the skull. 'That's . . . Scratch's lad, God rest that old cove's soul. That's . . . young Master Jack, who did vanish from these parts some twelve months or more ago . . . and no word from him since. Surely he isn't the one who . . . ? No. It cannot be.'

The coachman clambered down from his place and stretched to ease his spine. The top of his head felt sun-scorched, for all it was early morn. Two mucky boys had appeared, to see to the horses. He nodded to them, and threw a couple of coins.

'He's Jack Orion,' he told the tavern keeper. 'Musical genius, King Henry's pet. Gone up in the world faster than a firework. That's all I know.'

'Well, I'll be . . .' The keeper had recovered from his sprint across the yard, but not from the shock of seeing Old Scratch's boy returned, as if from the dead, and in such glorious style.

Boggle-eyed, he peered after Jack Orion (raising dust now, in the distance, from the heels of very good boots). Then he turned and told the coachman: 'It's the self-same Jack all right. Scratch always said the lad could carry a tune. But a genius? And known to the King? And to have been given so very much, just for a bit of fine fiddling ... well, well-a-day. I need a drink.'

The coachman said he could do with a sup himself, and would be wanting a bed for the night and somewhere safe from thieving rascals to store Orion's boxes.

'The ale we can provide,' the keeper replied. 'And safe storage, too, in our barn. But we have no bed to spare, friend, not tonight. Not with folk arriving from Salisbury for a wedding this afternoon, and our rooms already taken.'

'Never mind,' the coachman said. He would bed down in the barn, with the luggage. After all, he told himself, it was Hellish hot for April, and if he did start feeling chilly at some point in the night, well ... there was sure to be a fine fur cloak in one of Orion's boxes, and what was good enough for a jumped-up snot of a fiddle player, was good enough for him.

# XXIII

To get to the Huckles' house, Jack had to pass his own. He could have gone in for his first look around, for the stonemason was waiting in the cloister with a key the size of a pudding spoon. But he didn't. He raced on by.

*Later*, he thought to himself. *I will revel in all of this later. For until my Ja is with me to share in this great reward, Orion House might as well be made of cards, or slabs of marzipan.*

Still, he couldn't help but punch the air, triumphant, as he sprinted past the gates. Those holey men! Hah! He should have had them all tracked down and hauled back to bid him welcome. That inch worm, Day, in particular. It would have rubbed them all up raw—shirts or no shirts—to have had to call him 'sir'. Him. Jack the Lad. Cheese-seller of this parish.

It was priceless—beyond mirth—he thought, that the 'ramshackle' former monastery chosen for his reward had turned out to be this one. Had the King known? Had he remembered where Jack was from? Of course he had. The man was no fool. And, as he ran, Jack wished his sovereign good health, good mirth and a sixth wife with the sense, and grace, to leave other men alone.

Skirting the woods he saw bluebells, and winced to recall how he had gone bashing and lumbering among them less than a year ago. What a wretch he had been, back then. What a hapless fool.

He thought he might hear Sam Huckle's axe, biting into a tree, but the woods were eerily silent. Not even a cuckoo called.

The Huckles' gate was open, and there was no goose, this time, to hiss and go for his boots. Still, Jack paused awhile. He had been torn, earlier, between rolling up here in the carriage and arriving on foot. Now, standing all alone, and carrying only the precious fiddle that had earned him everything else, he felt such sweet elation that he knew he had made the right choice.

*I am Jack Orion* he told himself. *But I am also Jack the Lad, who has loved Janet Huckle all the days of his life, and needs no fine carriage at his back, as proof of it.*

## You're a fool. And a sight more hapless now than before, mark me.

*Shut up.*

Knocking, smartly, upon the Huckles' door, Jack wondered who might answer. Not the sight-addled sister, he hoped, for she would merely dither. And not the mother, either, for she wouldn't know him from Adam. Should Janet herself appear, he feared he might actually swoon. Best, he decided, that Sam Huckle should let him in.

But nobody came. Three times he knocked, each time louder than the last, and nobody answered that door.

Annoyed, he tried the latch. To his surprise, it lifted. Did they not fear, then, to be robbed? Or worse? Anger rippled through him, to think of this door left unsecured, with his Ja asleep upstairs, perhaps, and vulnerable to harm.

'Hello?' he called into the house.

No answer.

He stepped in, fastening the door behind him. Smells of baking, and wood, well-polished, reached him like the echo of a dream. There were flowers in pots upon the table—bluebells and cowslips and something white and lacy—and more flowers, twined in swags of ivy, all around the hearth, and up the ladder that led—Jack remembered now—to the bedchamber under the eaves.

Reaching out, he touched the table—stroked its well-worn surface as if it was a horse he had been fond of, long ago. *This is the table I hid under*, he remembered. *While she held my hands, and made the bad thoughts go away.*

*Well she's not here now. None of them are. So get thee back to London town and . . .*

*Quiet!*

Jack moved towards the ladder, intending—wanting—to go upstairs. To lie where his Ja had recently lain (he would know the place, he felt sure) and smell the scent of her on the bedding. *Just you wait, Ja, until you see our bed*, he thought. *It is, I'm told, as fine as any at Whitehall. As fine, perhaps, as the King's.*

He had one foot on the ladder, and was seeking a grip among the fuss of ivy and flowers, when he heard the thump of something landing on the floorboards overhead.

'*Ja?*'

The patter of footsteps, purposeful and quick, had him leaping away from the ladder, to stand, with a pumping heart and half-clenched fists, watching the gap between downstairs and up.

Then '*Yeeow!*' he cried, as some *thing* shot down the ladder, ran under the table and then jumped, with difficulty, onto a bench where it arched a warning with its back and fixed Jack with a malevolent stare.

It was a cat. An ancient female; six shades of grey.

'Hello,' Jack said to it. 'Remember me? No; nor I you.'

He looked to the ladder, and then away. He ought not to go up there after all, he realized. For it wouldn't really do for Sam Huckle to walk into his own house, to find someone in his daughter's bed—even if the daughter wasn't in it, herself, and even though that someone had a perfect right to be there.

*Where are you, Ja?* He wondered. *Why aren't you here?* Then he laid his hand once more upon the table, before heading for the door.

''Bye, bye puss,' he said. 'And don't look so smug. I'll be back.'

# XXIV

It was pleasant sitting in the cloister; at least the stonemason was finding it so. He could sense the dead there: the shades of holy men, slipping past, on their way to a chapel that was a dining hall, now.

Thinking himself among ghosts had never troubled the mason; for the dead, unlike the living, tended not to hang around. Dead monks, in particular, made excellent companions, being silent, for the most part, and unlikely to cut up rough.

Yet how those poor souls must be suffering, he thought, to have found their chapel so altered. For there were no angels any more in the big arched window, no choir screen smelling of age and incense, and no line of blue marble across the floor, marking the place where no woman might cross.

Where the altar had been was a sideboard, with legs just like a beast's. And should a tremulous ghost go searching in there for a chalice and holy water, he would grope and rummage in vain.

And where, oh where, those monks were bound to wonder, is our splinter from the Holy Cross?

Where indeed. The stonemason sighed and closed

his eyes for it had pained him—it really had—to learn that the monastery's precious relic, revered by pilgrims for nigh on four hundred years, had been hewn from an English oak.

And had he, himself, he wondered now, really seen that shadow—the shadow of the Holy cross—fall upon Orion's table? Perhaps, after all, it had just been a trick of the light.

And the chanting of plainsong in the dead of night? A dream, perhaps, that's all.

'Mason Barton?'

His eyes snapped open. The key to the house slid from his lap, and clattered on the cloister stones. 'Ah,' he said, scrambling to his feet. 'Mister Orion . . . sir. I didn't hear your carriage. Was I asleep?'

'Dunno,' Jack said. 'Is that my key?'

The mason tilted his head, the better to get the measure of this young sprig, in his fine black cloak and a cap with a curling feather. He lacks height, this Jack Orion, he thought. But that face . . . were I to sculpt that face in stone, and set it upon a shrine, it would be worshipped by all who chanced upon it. Young women in particular would come from miles around to . . .

'My key,' Jack repeated. 'Give it to me so I may hide it till it's needed.'

'But, sir . . .' The mason picked up the key and dusted it down on his apron. 'Are you not going straight in? You'll be wanting to inspect the work, surely, and . . .'

'Nah,' Jack said. 'I can do all of that later. Right now, I've a mind to eat at the tavern. After that, I must seek out Sam Huckle, for he is not at home.'

'Ah, yes,' said the mason, holding out the key. 'The wedding.'

Jack took the key.

'May your house never crumble, your hearth never cool and your door be open, always, to the faithful and the true,' intoned the mason.

'What wedding?' said Jack.

'Well now . . .' The mason breathed deep and willed himself to get this right; for Heaven forefend that Jack Orion should think him cloth-witted on this, their first acquaintance.

''Tis the daughter,' he said, with confidence. 'Sam Huckle's daughter is to be wed this afternoon. To his apprentice—a fine and honest craftsman, sir, who—'

'Which daughter?'

'Beg pardon, sir?'

'WHICH DAUGHTER?'

The mason flinched. Was there more than one? And why did it matter—for it clearly did. Alarmed, he trawled his memory . . . searching . . . searching . . . for the right information. Sam Huckle, he recalled, had spoken proudly, and often, of this wedding. But he, being not the slightest bit interested, had paid very little heed.

*Think*, he thought. *Think*. For Jack Orion's face had turned as white as salt, and the look in his eyes was awful.

The Huckle wife—whatever *her* name might be— was delighted with the match, Sam had definitely said that much, and had chuckled, too, adding that his wife—Hannah? Anna?—was not a woman to be easily pleased. And ... *what else* ... *what else had the carpenter said* ... ? Oh, yes ... yes ... that his daughter, his *youngest* girl ... that's right ... was so happy and excited that she had insisted on arranging all the wedding flowers herself, even though they would be a blur to her, on the day, as would her own pretty gown, and the faces of the guests ...

'It's the youngest one,' he said.

Jack let out his breath—slowly, as if it hurt. Then he grabbed the stonemason by the shoulders and looked him full in the face. 'Are you *absolutely sure?*' he said, each word separate and precise.

'Yes,' the mason answered, squirming as the key in Jack's left hand pressed into him. 'I'm sure. She's half-blind sir, if it helps you to know it. And small, for her age. And her name ...' his voice faltered, then rallied itself: 'Her name beings with a "D" ... Dora-Joan ... Dorcas-Jane ...'

'Hah!' Jack let go of the mason's shoulders. Then he threw his key high into the air and caught it coming down. 'Hurrah and hurrah again,' he crowed. 'It's a young enough bride she'll be, but a lucky one too, don't you think? I'm guessing Sam Huckle hired that apprentice with this marriage already in mind. Marry the ditherer; take her off

171

my hands, and I'll teach you all I know. Hah—what merry sport!'

'Yes, sir,' said the mason, faintly. 'What merry sport indeed.'

'I'll take myself off to church, then,' Jack told him. 'To wish the bride and groom good chance. They will be kin of mine 'ere long, so best we all make friends.'

Happy, now, he looked properly, and for the first time, at the front of Orion House. At his sturdy oak door. At the glass, glinting, cheekily, in his windows. At the two 'J's, intertwined. And if the souls of holey men were swirling into the place, or leaving it, appalled, he neither saw nor sensed them.

'It is well done,' he said to the stonemason. 'I— we—could ask for nothing better.'

# XXV

Tables and benches for the wedding feast had been set up in a meadow, a five minute walk up from the church. Jack, who had expected the celebration to be at the market place, or in the tavern yard, was surprised.

He had gone straight to the church. The door had been closed, so he had stood some way away from it, with the sun hot on his back, and a sudden shyness in his heart which turned, as he stood there, to unease.

Should he go in or should he not?

He wanted to go in. He longed to see his Ja—to catch her eye and watch the blush rise in her face. But something was stopping him. Not bad thoughts. He wasn't having those. He just knew, without knowing how, that to enter this place, under any circumstance, would make him sorrowful at best and, at worst, rather ill.

The marriage service had already begun for he could hear the priest intoning, loud and clear, that if anyone present knew of some impediment to this union he should speak it now or forever keep his peace.

'She can't see,' he mouthed. 'She'll trip over your feet and drop your babies in the fire.' Chuckling at his own wit made him feel a great deal better. There was no need, he decided, to interrupt the service. Instead, he would find somewhere else to wait—somewhere pleasant, beyond the shadow of this church where he might sit, unnoticed, to feast his eyes upon his Ja as soon as she appeared.

*Are you sad, Ja?* He aimed this thought, like the beam of a lantern, at the closed church door. *Are you wondering where in the world I am, and to what purpose, that you must see your little sister married before you are? Well I'm here! I've come home! And I will be by your side before this hour is through, and for all the hours, and days, and months and years to come thereafter, in this life and beyond.*

## You blinkered fool. You numbskull.

Annoyed, Jack looked up and away from the church. He saw the tables in the meadow; recognized the fripperies—the swags of ivy along each table's length; the yellow, white and blue of flowers. *Had I known, before, about this,* he thought, *they could have set all that up at Orion House. It would have been my pleasure to host this wedding feast. But then, I probably own the meadow, so . . .*

It was a relief, for him, to turn away from the church; to let go conviction that stepping inside would have made him retch, or weep. This was going to pose a problem, he realized, on his own wedding day, but he would cross that bridge when he came to it.

The climb to the meadow made him pant, and sweat, but the breeze up there was delicious, and the view a feast for the eyes. Jack had never thought to miss this place, but gazing now across valleys, fields and woodland . . . at the lake away to his left and the Tor away to his right . . . he knew himself a country lad, and lucky to be so.

Alone, for now, among the wedding tables, Jack stood for a long time looking out across the land. Idly, as if it didn't really matter, he focused on the spot where he'd guessed the old goat shed ought to be, along with what passed for a dwelling. He couldn't find them. They had gone. Or maybe he'd got it wrong, and they were further along the ridge, or hidden by trees. Perhaps . . .

A burst of laughter made him jump, and spin around, and he grinned to see two red-faced lads rolling a barrel into the meadow. Behind them came four lasses bearing platters of meat, cheese and bread. The girls were laughing at the boys—at their pantings, and their pushings, and the way their rear ends bobbed.

'Is that all for me?' Jack quipped and the girls laughed some more, and the boys puffed and mumbled—*What, sir? No, sir. Some of it, sir. Good day, sir. It's from the tavern, sir, for the wedding feast.* —and he let them all get on with it, while he chose the best place to be, to wait for his Ja. For was that the sound of . . . ? Yes. It was. The church bells were ringing. Any moment now, his Ja would be climbing where he had climbed, and then she would appear.

He considered running from the meadow to meet her; pictured himself scooping her up in his arms and whirling her round and round. But running downhill might not be wise. Too fast and he might crash into old mother Huckle, or knock the little bride clean off her feet. He might drop, and break his fiddle, and that would never do. No. He would leave this section of the meadow, he decided, and walk further up the hill. From there, he would see Janet coming, before she saw him. From there, he would savour the moment.

# XXVI

It had been a beautiful service, everyone agreed, and hadn't they been lucky with the weather?

'It's a granny you'll be by next spring,' Kate Bundy said to Annie, as they left the church. 'I'd bet my spindle on it.'

'Give them a chance!' Annie answered, happily. 'They have plenty of time for that. They have all the time in the world . . .' And so it did seem, with the sky so blue, and the air so warm and everyone so merry as they mingled awhile, then got themselves in order for the clamber up the hill.

'Ooh, I'm getting too old for this,' puffed Kate, hanging on to Annie's arm as the path steepened towards the meadow. 'And my left foot, Annie, has been playing me up something dreadful. Goes stone dead on me, it does, for no reason I can fathom. I won't be dancing later, that's for sure.'

'None of us will,' Annie reminded her. 'Unless that good for nothing cousin of yours recovers enough from his heavings to come up and play us a tune. A bad oyster? Hah! 'Tis the ale that addles that rascal so. Have you seen him yet today? Up and trousered, that is?'

Kate admitted that she hadn't. 'Oh, but I'm looking forward to the feast,' she added, by way of changing the subject. 'Beef and mustard, my Alice said we're having. Beef and mustard, and enough ale to float a warship. You've done your girl proud, Annie. Her and her lovely man.'

'Thank you,' said Annie and then: 'Sam!' She called ahead. 'Sam Huckle, slow down. It's a mischief you'll be doing yourself, charging ahead so. He wants everything perfect up there,' she excused him, to Kate. 'Everything.'

Kate slid, let out a little shriek, and clutched tighter to Annie's arm 'That was a slug I just trod on,' she said. 'Be it good luck or bad, to kill a slug, Annie Huckle?'

'Good,' Annie told her. 'On a wedding day, at least.'

They could see the four tavern girls, now—Kate's daughter, Alice, and her friends—holding aloft the willow arch, one girl at each corner.

'So pretty.' Kate sighed. 'Such a pretty arch, with the cowslips and the ivy and all.'

'Dorigan fashioned it,' Annie told her. 'She was determined.'

'May the Lord bless and keep that child,' Kate murmured. And, 'They're coming! They're coming!' came the shout from close behind, and both the women had to scramble, then—'like a couple of old hens!' laughed Annie—as others ran to overtake them . . . to beat the newlyweds through the arch.

The youngest guests were banging basins and pots with sticks and spoons, and flinging white blossoms around. 'Run! Run!' they called to Kate and Annie, through a blizzard of falling petals. 'They're right behind us. Hurry!'

For a fleeting moment, before ducking to enter the arch, Annie saw her husband—through already, and looking for her, with worry all over his face.

*Something has happened*, she thought. *Something has gone wrong. Is the ale sour? Is there not enough beef to go round? Have those giddy girls forgotten to carry up the mustard?*

And, 'Who is *that*?' she heard Kate Bundy exclaim before Kate, too, was under the arch, in a six-second limbo of scent, and shade, and dangling tendrils of green.

Lurching out into the meadow—catching, and tearing the sleeve of her gown in her hurry to be through—Annie grabbed her husband's waiting hand. 'What is it, Sam? What's happened?'

Pulling her to his side, Sam looked away up the hill. His hand, in hers was shaking. 'You're not to fuss,' he said. 'You're not to worry at all. I'll deal with it.'

Following his gaze, Annie saw a pale-face youth, in a cloak and feathered cap. He was standing very still, looking down upon the arch. *Oh no*, she thought. *No, no, no . . . Not now. Not today. It cannot be . . .*

'Be that Jack Orion?' gasped Kate Bundy, who was blocking the exit from the willow arch, with her big fat behind, and leering up the hill. 'Or Old Scratch's boy, cleaned up?'

'Both!' her daughter called, from the corner of the arch. 'But he's Jack Orion now, all right, for he has told us so. And it does please him, he says, to stay for the feast and to pay for it too, when it's done.'

'Well-a-day!' chortled Kate, ignoring, for the moment, the entreaties of the young, who were piling up behind her, unable to leave the arch. 'You were right, Annie Huckle. To squash a slug stone-dead on a wedding day is truly a fortunate thing.'

'It's him, isn't it?' Annie said to Sam. *'What is he doing here?'*

'Hush, dear. I said I'd deal with it.'

'Deal with it?' Annie had to close her eyes. She couldn't look at Sam, or at Kate, and certainly not at that ... *person* ... come from the Devil only knew where, to spoil this perfect day. 'Sam Huckle,' she said, through gritted teeth, 'you couldn't deal with a fly on the bread without begging its pardon first. You couldn't ...'

But: 'Hurrah and good health to the newlyweds!' the four tavern girls cried out. And Annie had no choice but to hold her tongue and open her eyes. For Kate Bundy had finally shifted herself; the others were all through, and nothing, *nothing*, was going to spoil this moment as young Dorigan, in a pretty new gown, stepped, beaming, out of the arch, followed by the bride and groom.

Sam Huckle felt a tear roll down his cheek. *This*, he told himself, *is all that matters. Only this.* Then Annie gave him a nudge and he quickly cleared his throat.

'By all the graces,' he called out, as custom demanded he should. 'I present to all within this space the Lord and Lady of our wedding feast: Thomas and Janet Day.'

# XXVII

*No.*

*No. N . . . n . . . n . . . n . . .*

Jack could not have said how long he sat there on the grass. For sit he did, thinking only to wait . . . to let time stand still . . . until that **blow-fly Sam Huckle** and his **congregation of ditch-born jesters** saw fit to admit that *none of this was real*. That they had *planned the whole charade*.

Perhaps, he thought . . . *n . . . n . . . no.* Not perhaps, it was actually highly likely . . . the stonemason . . . *y . . . yes . . . that's right . . .* had let it be known in the tavern that Jack Orion had arrived, and was coming to the wedding. *The younger girl's wedding. The blind girl's wedding. The girl whose name starts with 'D'.*

*And then . . . and then . . .* somebody else, one of the tavern girls perhaps . . . *no, definitely one of those girls . . .* had s . . . s . . . said guesswhatguesswhat? That fine young gentleman, sitting up yonder, was the ch . . . cheese-seller, once. **And now . . . and now?** Those H . . . H . . . Huckles . . . and all those others . . . were set on reminding him—*and why not?*

182

—that even a favourite of the King's could be brought back down to size by a gentle blow **a savage cut more like** to the heart.

Well, ha-ha.

'All right!' he wanted to scream, while running pell-mell down the hill. 'All right. You've had your fun. Now stop it.'

But his voice wouldn't work. And his legs wouldn't work. Only his mind was working, it seemed: laying out what he had just witnessed and cutting bits away until it was something he could look at without wanting his heart to stop.

That sister. That Dorigan. Everything about her, as she'd jumped from the wedding tunnel, had been too wild, he decided—too *ecstatic*—to be anything but a newlywed's demeanour. And those newly-weds, *so-called*, had not been holding hands when they themselves emerged, only chuckling, like two people in on a mischief.

And the bride, *so-called*, had picked something—a flower, he thought—from her hair, exclaiming to find the hair and the thing so tightly meshed, although of course they were . . . of course . . . because didn't her pretty hair always go to tangles, in the slightest breeze?

And any new husband worth his salt would have untangled that flower himself, unable to resist a reason, big or small, to touch this lovely girl, who now belonged to him.

And Day hadn't done that.

He hadn't even looked.

And yes . . . of *course*. Here was the biggest flaw in the whole masquerade. Thomas Day was a holey man was he not? Committed, still—surely?—to chastity, poverty and a life as dull as sludge, despite what had become of the monasteries, and the old holey ways.

A farce, Jack told himself. This was—is—a farce. And they must think me some cloth-wit, to be completely taken in. Well, they may have their sport a while longer. I can wait.

*Go on then*, he dared the bad voice. *You're very quiet. Have your say, for what it's worth.*

But, so far as he could tell, only his own thoughts continued to whirr as the wedding guests took their places, for the feast. And as he watched, that . . . that botch of nature . . . that beardless swain, Day, led she who was not his to lead, OR EVEN DARE TO LOOK UPON, to a place at the top table, he swore that he would knock the wretch down and kick ten bells and a Hail Mary out of him, as soon as he got the chance.

*You have taken this too far, Brother Day*, he thought. *It has gone beyond a joke.*

'Go and speak to him, husband,' Annie Huckle said to Sam. 'Tell him to go away. For I cannot eat a morsel knowing him to be up there, staring down. Indeed, I cannot even breathe in comfort.'

Sam Huckle looked hunted. He had been keeping his back to young Master Jack hoping against hope that, the next time he checked, the boy would have disappeared. He was watching his beloved Jannie, and his fine apprentice—his son-in-law now—taking their places at the table. Having eyes only for each other, they had yet to notice Jack Orion, sitting on the hill.

Jack Orion.

Orion House.

It made Sam's face burn, and then go cold to think of those two Js, intertwined. How carefully he and Thomas Day had carved those things. How sincerely they had wished long lives and happiness to Orion and his lady love as they fixed both letters, securely, above the great oak door.

'Maybe . . .' he appealed to his wife. 'Perhaps . . . the boy is best left alone. What harm, after all, is he doing? It is hardly a hanging offence, wife, for a person to sit on a hilltop, enjoying the afternoon sun.'

'Sam Huckle,' Annie answered. '*Deal with it!*'

And then young Alice Bundy was leaning over their shoulders, serving slices of beef, only not very well, for she kept twisting her head round, to smile, hopefully, up the hill.

'Should I take him up something to eat?' she asked. 'After all, he did say . . .'

'No, Alice. Leave him be.'

The sharpness of her mother's tone made Dorigan Huckle look up. Left, right and up and down she looked, seeing only face-shapes and flower-smudges and a melting together of land and sky, but sensing danger all the same. 'Mother?' she called, softly. 'Father?' And then Janet looked up too and saw, for the first time, the figure on the hill.

'Oh!' she exclaimed. 'Is that Jack up there? Our Jack, I mean, as used to live with us? Dorigan ... sweetheart ... don't be a goose, sit down. Why, he looks so fine! I love the hat. Surely he and Jack Orion cannot be one and the same. Are they? Is it true? Thomas ... Father ... whatever's wrong?'

# XXVIII

It was Thomas Day who insisted that Jack be invited down, and made welcome. It was his wedding day after all—the happiest day of his life—so he had goodwill enough to share; even with Old Scratch's tetchy foundling.

'Go and fetch him, Sam,' he bade his father-in-law. 'Before the beef is all gone. And have him sit at our table. I, for one, am agog to know how he came by his great fortune.'

'Me too,' chimed Janet.

*No* whispered Dorigan, moving so close to her father, and scrabbling so urgently at his side that it seemed to Sam Huckle that, had she claws instead of fingernails—this strange, beloved child—she would have torn straight through his shirt, burrowed deep into his flesh, and hidden herself away beneath his ribs.

'It's all right, Dorrie,' he whispered, planting a kiss on top of her head. 'Be a good girl.'

'Dorigan!' Annie's voice came out fiercer than intended. 'This is your sister's marriage feast. Would you spoil it for her, with your antics? Move back to your own place. *Now.*'

'Do as your mother bids, child,' Sam murmured. And Dorigan Huckle slid away, knowing herself lost, now, to the danger—the terrible threat—that nobody else could see coming.

'Annie?' Sam lowered his voice, and his gaze, too, lest something in his wife's face should make him feel more of a clod, and a useless cove, than he already did. 'Shall I fetch him down, then, instead of sending him away? Don't you think, dear . . . isn't it possible . . . that he might be civil to us all?'

Annie shrugged, raised her cup, and took a swig of ale.

'Oh, do fetch him!' begged young Alice, come to dollop out the mustard. 'For he does look so very lonesome, crouched all by himself.'

'Annie?'

Annie Huckle took another drink. 'You must do as you will, husband,' she said. 'But if it's civility you're wanting for the rest of the afternoon, don't sit him next to me.'

Jack saw Sam Huckle coming and began shivering anew. *Hah*, he thought, gritting his teeth. *Now we're getting somewhere. Now we'll see how this jolly jape shall fizzle out.* Still, his body continued to shake and his teeth to chatter in his mouth as if it was snow and ice he sat upon, on a winter's afternoon.

'Jack?' said Sam, as soon as he was sure of being heard.

188

'That-t-t's . . . m . . . m-me.'

Sam stopped and stood very still. There was a lot of grass remaining, between himself and the shivering boy, but he preferred, for the moment, not to cross it. 'Are you unwell?' he asked.

*Unwell? Hah! No. Only teased, Sam Huckle,* **beyond endurance.** *Only treated* **like more of a fool than I have ever deserved to be taken for.**

'N-no,' he replied. 'Not I.'

'Well then . . . will you come down with me, and join the feast?'

'Why?'

Sam swallowed a sigh. Because, he thought, you are here now and I dare not send you away. Because once you were a helpless scrap, who slept upon my shoulder. Because I did not keep my word to you, and am frightened that it matters.

'Because we—the family—all wish it,' he said.

'All, sir? Is that t-truly how it is? Well then, I'm with you. Help me up. Mind the fiddle.'

Confused, Sam stepped forward and held out both his hands. Jack's grasp made him flinch—the boy's fingers were ice-cold. 'Are you certain you are well?' he said, as Jack hauled himself upright. 'For if . . .'

'Enough,' Jack said. 'I'm hungry now. Let's go.' And as his feet took him down, towards the celebration, it seemed to Jack that he slipped into a dream; the kind in which the people you encounter are known to you

189

and yet not. In which all that is said, and all that is done, is tinged with just enough peculiarity to let you know, on some deep level, that none of this matters. None of it is real.

All the guests applauded, women and girls loudest of all, as Jack (head down, eyes lowered) drew near. *Ah, bless him*, some of the women thought. *He's gone all shy!* And there were calls of 'Welcome home, Master Jack,' and 'Bring ale for Jack Orion.' *Ah yes*, Jack thought, still looking at his boots. *Jack Orion. That's me. And, yes, I have come home. And, yes, thank you, I will take a cup of ale.*

'There's a place for you here, sir,' one of the tavern girls called out.

*So there is*, he thought, and sat in it. 'What's your name, sweetheart?' he asked the girl, keeping his eyes on the table . . . on the meat under his nose.

'I'm Alice Bundy, sir,' she said. 'We did meet, sir, earlier on. And I recall you, from the market. Would you like me to take that for you?'

She meant his fiddle. She was inviting him to unstrap the fiddle, lift it over his head, and deliver it into her keeping. As if he could. As if he had either the strength, or the will, to do something as ordinary as that. 'No,' he said. 'The fiddle stays with me. We are joined.'

Alice laughed, doubtfully, and asked if he wanted some mustard.

'You know what, Alice,' he told her, 'I have a perfect craving for mustard. It is the one thing—*the only thing*—I missed while I was away. Bring me a whole dish of the stuff.'

And still, he would not look up.

'This meat looks good,' he said, and attacked it with his knife.

'Aren't you going to wait for your mustard?' he heard someone say as he wolfed the whole meal down.

'Nope,' he replied, through a half-chewed mouthful. 'For a person will wait only so long, for whatever it is he craves. Then, alas and alack, he must make do.'

For a moment or two there was silence. A puzzled one, Jack sensed, but that was all right. He wasn't at court any more, among sharp and learned minds. People's wits turned more slowly here. They needed time to work things out. And the beef really was very good.

Then: 'You have done well for yourself, Jack,' Thomas Day said. 'Old Scratch would have been proud, God rest his soul.'

'What's that?'

There was grease all around Jack's mouth and coursing down his chin, but he didn't bother wiping it away. Lifting his gaze he looked, not at Thomas Day, on the opposite bench, but at the sky above Thomas's head. And he kept his eyes fixed on that spot, while Thomas recounted how the old man had died, three days after Jack's leaving. Peacefully. At the monastery. A palsy, no doubt, as he had complained, before passing, of a great unshiftable heaviness in his head.

'The goats are thriving,' Day continued, 'Jannie and I have moved them, for our own convenience—their shed, and your old home, being fit to fall, as they since have—but they are yours to do with as you will. And Scratch left to you his savings. They are of little account but . . . well . . . oh, and the handkerchief that belonged to your mother.'

'I washed it,' said Janet. 'The handkerchief I mean, for it was in a sorry state. And I have kept it safe and clean, so if Thomas and I may visit Orion House one day, I will bring it to you, in my pocket.'

There was a cloud, up in the sky, that looked, to Jack a lot like a goat. Not a sheep . . . no . . . definitely a goat, for it had a beardy-looking bit trailing from it. And . . . yes . . . here came another one. It was enough to make even a wretch—even the sorriest of wretches—smile. *Mollykins* Jack thought. *Lavender. Sidney. Old Trot.* If he could remember all of their names, everything would be . . .

**Jannie and I, said he. Thomas and I, said she. Sprites and fires boy . . . are you really so dim-witted?**

Jack blinked.

Then he looked at Janet.

She met his gaze kindly, and he felt his heart contract. 'You have your mother's eyes,' she told him. 'Old Scratch said so. When he knew that he must die he asked Tom to tell you—should you ever return to this place—that he believed your mother loved you, and would have missed you all her days. But you were not her husband's child, and . . . well . . . she was only human. He wished for you to know this, and not to mind.'

Jack nodded. He was drinking in her face. Her sweet, beloved face. 'Thank you,' he said. 'Interesting.'

'You're welcome,' she replied and Jack took the smile she bestowed upon him as a great, and wonderful, sign. *It's not hopeless*, he thought, then. *It may seem so, but it's not. Day might think he has her, but he's wrong. She has treasured my mother's handkerchief. She wants to come to my house. There is something very wrong here, but it rests not with her, or me.*

Overcome, he looked away. Along to the right he looked, not taking anything in; just needing time to compose himself, while hope did its false work. A few of the guests, thinking to have his attention, quit their bantering and raised their cups of ale.

'Will you play for us later, sir?' Kate Bundy called, across the space between the tables. 'For my cousin is a-bed with a spring fever, and cannot do the honours.'

Jack inclined his head, to shut her up, and turned the other way. His gaze fell upon Annie Huckle, reaching for her cup. She caught him looking and froze; defiance and fear tussling on her face.

193

*My ring,* he thought, then. *You kept it from her, didn't you? You never told her I'd be back. That's why she agreed to wed another. THAT'S WHY DAY IS BESIDE HER, NOW, WHEN . . . WHEN . . .*

'Pray excuse me,' he said to no one in particular. Then he got up from his place and strolled to the table's end.

'A word,' he said, bending so close to Annie's ear that the feather in his cap brushed the lightest of caresses down her cheek.

Behind him all was chatter and the clinking of cups. Only Sam Huckle, who was closest, leaned anxiously in to say: 'Jack—please. This is not the time.' The younger daughter, Jack noticed, was clinging to him like a wart.

*Time . . .* he thought, dreamily. *What has time got to do with any of this? With me? With her? We'll have all the time in the world, once a few misunderstandings have been all cleared up.*

'Be still, husband,' Annie Huckle said, and then rose, steadily enough, to her feet. 'Come,' she bade Jack. 'Come with me.'

# XXIX

*Ho hum*, Jack thought. Then: *Dandelion, Dainty, and Trot.*

But the clouds above his head were racing now; the bits of blue in between like the tatters of something gorgeous. And however many times he looked up he couldn't find his goats, for they had morphed into something else. Something bigger, no longer a joke.

'The sun will soon be gone,' Annie said, without turning round. 'But we certainly had the best of it. And the tavern did us proud, after all. I did think to serve lamb, it being the season, but my Sam said no, Annie, let's have the beef. He does so love a slice of beef, my Sam ...'

Her voice was a lullaby. Jack would have liked it not to end. He would have been almost content, he realized, to keep on walking; through meadow grass and cowslips ... past the tavern and the church ... on and on, as far Salisbury, and beyond, with his fiddle on his back, peace and quiet in his head, and the sing-song lilt of this woman's voice telling him that all was well, in his life ... in this place ... in this world.

Only it wasn't.

At the very edge of the meadow, where grass gave way to earth, fresh-turned, Annie stopped walking and let her voice wind down. What to do? What to say next, to this . . . this . . . ? Her thoughts flew, over the meadow, beyond the church and away to the sun-warmed wall in her own back garden where the ring with the blood-coloured stone still was. She pictured it in its crevice, neatly hidden but as potent, still, and as dangerous, as a wasp can be, when riled. Not lost for ever, though. Not gone to the bottom of the lake. He could have it back, if he wanted, to give to another girl.

For a long moment Annie considered the horizon, as if drawing strength from it. Then she turned herself around and looked Jack full in the face. 'I cared for you,' she said. 'I suckled you, and nursed you, and 'tis as certain as next Monday week that I actually saved your life.'

'So?' He held her gaze for a moment, then considered the rest of her face, seeking traces, there, of Janet. *Around the nose, perhaps,* he thought. *But nowhere else.*

'So I would ask you to bear that in mind, child, when I tell you this: I did not allow our Jannie to have, or even to know about, your ring.'

*I am not a child, Mother Huckle. I am Jack the Lad. Jack Orion to you. I am the bad Ja and she is the good and we needed no ring, to make us sure, only peace, and time, and to be left well alone by interfering ... meddling old ...* I AM ILL-USED, MADAM! I AM . . . MOST CRUELLY . . . MOST WICKEDLY DECEIVED . . .

'Let. Me. Be.' He would have sucked together all the juices in his mouth and spat the words right at her; only he was not a child. He was Jack Orion.

Annie Huckle gasped. She had drunk more ale than was good for her, and though her step, and her speech, remained steady, she felt more than usually invincible. And that made her stupid. Leave? She actually giggled. Well fa-la-la. He had taken on some pretty airs, this foundling of hers, during his time away.

And handsome. By the saints, he was a good-looking boy. Even now, with his face turned, haughtily, away from her and his mouth a bitter line, he put her in mind of angels. Of the ones in the monastery window—only, of course, they were no longer there.

'You're angry,' she said. 'And your pride has taken a dent. But it will pass. Look at you: grown so bonny, and risen so high in this world. It will be a lucky lass who wins your heart, Jack, one of these fine days.'

*Hah!* Jack wheeled around so suddenly that Annie threw up her hands, thinking him about to fall . . . preparing, if she must, to catch him. But he had only turned his back on her and now he was striding away. Back to the celebration . . . towards her family.

Taken off guard, she let him go. Then: 'You are to behave yourself, I hope,' she called, doing her best to catch him up, but too hampered by her skirts, and by the effects of too much ale, to match his stride. 'For the fondness you surely bear us . . . all of us . . . for taking you in . . . we want no trouble this day . . . do you hear?'

Kate Bundy saw Jack coming, and waved and called 'Yoo-hoo!' She, too, had drunk more ale than was good for her. The tables, Jack noticed, had been moved away and some of the guests had gone. Those who remained had formed themselves into a haphazard circle and had been waiting, he could tell, for . . . well . . . for him.

He drew nearer . . . and nearer still. Not believing, any more, that this was all some merry jape; but holding tight and fast to the distinct possibility . . . the almost certain truth . . . that his Ja had only married Day, because, thanks to **that conniving witch,** her mother, she had thought her own dear Ja lost to her, for ever, and not missing her at all.

*Where are you Ja? Where? For we can sort this out.*

When his eyes found her, among the guests, he had to stop and stand quite still while delight rippled through him, in wave after wave after wave. 'Don't you utter another word to me,' he cautioned Annie Huckle, as she came panting up behind him. 'Go back to your husband. I know to behave.'

Left alone, he fell to wondering how quickly, and on what grounds, he could get this marriage annulled.

It seemed a travesty to him, now—a crime and a sin—that a former monk could marry anyone at all. Day, he decided, was worse than any heretic for he had broken his vows, like pie crusts.

*Look at me*, he willed Janet. *Now! Look at me now!* And she did. She turned just once, to wave at him, and then went to find her husband. And when she found Thomas Day, conversing with her sister, she slipped her arms around his waist and stood herself on tiptoe, to gently kiss the back of his neck. And Thomas, who had not seen or heard her coming swung slowly round to face her, and she beamed up at him, and he smiled, delighted, down at her, and Jack Orion watched it all, his mind a total blank.

'Will you play for us, sir? Before it gets dark?'

Alice Bundy was a plumpish girl, with bold green eyes. She reminded Jack, a bit, of Joan Bulmer.

'Did you know, Alice,' he said. 'That Katherine Howard—Queen Katherine, that is—did ask, on the eve of her execution, for the block to be brought to her? In the Tower?'

Alice pulled a face. 'No, sir, I didn't, sir. Why ever would she ask for such a thing?'

'I heard tell,' he replied, 'that she wanted to make a trial of it—to know how best to place herself. The blow was coming, Alice, and she wished to be prepared.'

'That's gruesome, sir,' Alice declared. 'Indeed, I would rather not dwell on it.'

And: 'Jack!' Thomas Day called out. 'Won't you play us a tune on that fiddle of yours? For there is light enough, still, for dancing, and my wife . . .' he paused for a kiss . . . no, two kisses . . . and a round of applause from the guests . . . 'My wife . . . my Jannie . . . does dearly love to dance.'

'No,' Jack said, just loud enough to be heard.

But 'Please, sir!' and 'Ah, go on,' the guests cried out. And Kate Bundy promised him a fresh-bought honeycomb if he would only fiddle a jig. And one of the men did laugh at that, and splutter something crude. And Sam Huckle, although distracted by the tuggings of his younger daughter—who was saying, 'Please father . . . please . . . may we not go home?'—said: 'It would be nice, Jack, if you would.'

So, 'Dance, then,' Jack Orion said, and reached for his fiddle. Thomas Day wasn't much of a dancer. Still, he threw himself into it, for he wanted to please his wife. And, *Look at her*, Jack thought. *Just look at my Jannie, dancing like a faerie queen . . . like a sunbeam on a wall.*

And, 'Come on, Annie,' Sam said to his wife, giving her waist a squeeze. 'Let's dance. You too Dorrie—I'll guide you, don't you fret. For just listen how that boy can play; how he makes those wires sing . . .'

And then everyone was dancing. And Jack began to sweat. Lower he bent, and lower still as his bow flew over the strings and his boots stamped time on the grass.

200

He tipped off his feathered cap. He shrugged off his fine, dark cloak. And he did both of these things without missing a single note.

**That's it, boy . . . that's it. They're whirling like dervishes now. Play faster!**

*Faster? Yes. I can do that. I can play so fast . . . so well . . . that it will drive young women wild. I have made a Queen laugh, and a King cry with the tunes that I can play . . .*

**And don't you loathe this prancing crowd, my sweet? This multitude of fools?**

*Oh yes, I most certainly do.*
**Don't you wish every one of them ill?**

*Oh yes, I wish all of them ill.*
**Then play faster, Jack Orion, and faster . . . faster still!**

Kate Bundy felt it first. The deadening of her feet Not just the one that always dragged, but the other one as well. *I believe I must stop and rest*, she thought, and stop she very soon did. Thomas Day felt it as a tightening in his chest and reached out for his Jannie. Dorigan Huckle began to run, in her own kind of way, and got as far as the edge of the meadow. Sam and Annie Huckle went together, with Annie wondering aloud why her legs felt like two anchors, suddenly, and her arms much the same, and Sam shaking, kindly, the lead-weight of his head and saying, 'Wife, I do believe, we have supped too much . . .'

Alice Bundy and her friends had been spinning in a line . . . fast enough to make their skirts rise up . . . fast enough, they hoped, to catch Jack Orion's eye . . . and all that they knew, before stopping, was that their skirts had become too heavy to rise, as if their mothers, or other spoil-their-funs, had sewn pebbles in the hems.

Janet was the last to go. On tiptoe she went, with her arms raised and her wedding ring glinting in the setting of the sun. Once, twice, it flashed . . . and then no more.

# XXX

*Ha!* Jack dropped his bow, and then his fiddle, hard upon the ground. *That's shown you,* he thought. *That's shown you, has it not? No one crosses Jack Orion; no one breaks his heart, or a promise that they made, or makes him look a fool. And never . . . never, ever again, do you hear me?* **Do you hear?** *should he be made to play for his supper.*

Then he threw himself down on the grass, and waited, shaking, for something to happen. When nothing did . . . when the haphazard circle of standing stones remained exactly that, he began to scream.

# XXXI

Dawn broke. It was going to be another lovely day. Jack didn't want to move; wasn't sure he could, for there was no feeling in his feet, and his fingers had gone blue. *Perhaps I'm about to join them*, he thought, and it was the first and only scrap of consolation to have sounded in his head since he had looked up from his playing, and seen what he had done.

After a while, he cleared his throat. Then he sneezed—he couldn't help it. How loud it sounded . . . his own *atishoo* . . . and how awful, and odd, it was that no one called out afterwards: 'Bless you, sir,' or, 'A tish, a tash, young Master Jack, and may you always prosper.'

The new light hurt his eyes, but then he had yet to close them. For hours, now, he had been watching the stones. The moon had helped with that, and he wished, now, that she had stayed.

He had counted the stones a countless number of times. There were thirty-two altogether, he thought, including the one by the meadow's edge, which, to begin with, he had missed. He had calculated their heights and weights and tried just by looking—for he really could not move—to see some resemblance in them to actual folk. But he couldn't. There was none.

'Where are you?' he whispered now, through lips as blue as his fingers. 'Where have you gone?' And it wasn't just his Ja he was thinking of, it was all of them. He counted the stones again; aloud, this time, as if the sound of his voice might somehow break the spell.

And, *Sound* . . . he thought, dizzily. *Could it work? Surely it might. For if I made them go, with the songs my fiddle can sing, I can surely bring them back in the same way.*

His fiddle was slick with dew. *Work*, he willed it, and staggered to his feet. He felt the urge to bow. To the stones. So he did. And then he set the fiddle, firm and cold, beneath his chin and began, very softly, to play.

He played a cradle song to begin with, as if to soothe a fractious child, or an unhappy King. He played of sheep in the meadow, and cows in the corn, and of daddy gone a-hunting, but coming back soon. He played of the morning that was breaking, just like the first morning, and of blackbirds that were singing, just like the first bird. And then he raised the fiddle higher, and with it the bow, and played of wedding bells pealing through the soft, spring air and of happy people dancing, and then going home.

And it made not the slightest bit of difference.

* * *

205

*It wasn't my fault. I didn't plan it. It wasn't my fault. It wasn't.*

*Time, Ja, is a peculiar thing—at least, I find it so. Whole weeks slip by without significance, becoming months that pile up behind me and cannot be told apart. Exactly how much time has passed, I wonder, since I . . . since you . . . ? A year? More?*

*I am astonished to think that it might be more, as it so very easily could. It is as if I have slept through countless seasons, and tides, and the comings and goings of our moon, without knowing the why or the what of myself. And who knows? Perhaps I have. I sleep a lot, Ja. As much as I can. All day and into the night. If I must wake, I decided, a long time ago, let it be while others rest for I no longer care to go among ordinary folk, in the bright light of day.*

*This works, most of the time. Yet there are days—and this is one—when sleep eludes me. When seconds seem eternal, and memories fill my head to bursting. Good memories and bad. Sunbeams and poison. On days like this, I have longed for death the way I used to long for you.*

*'So die, then,' I hear you say, your voice a sad, sweet echo. Well, my lost and only love, don't think I haven't tried. Don't imagine for a moment I felt entitled to carry on breathing after what I did to you. And to the others—I*

don't forget the others, for all they meant
nothing to me. For pity's sake, Ja, I turned you
all to stone. It is the stuff of sorcery . . . of tales
told to frighten children on All Souls' Eve. It
is as strange as it is awful and so beyond the
bounds of human understanding that I would
have laughed in the face of anyone who had
foreseen it.

'So die then . . .'

Hah!

The Old Man used to say I had the Devil's
own luck, and the Devil's rude health to boot.
He said it so often it grew tedious. 'Change the
tune, old man,' I used to snap at him, 'before my
ears do shrink from boredom and drop clean off
my head.'

Oh Ja, if I had only known . . .

I tried to bring you back. I would have given
anything—tried anything—to undo what I had
done. But when it came clear to me that there
was nothing to be gained by trying, or wishing,
or waiting, I ran. Without stopping. To the lake
beyond your father's house.

The water, that morning, was calm, with a mist
rising from it, like steam. The sky above was as
blue as your eyes and I howled—yes I did—to
think of those eyes, and of every other part of
you, stopped, or trapped, or vanished I knew
not where.

First, I threw the fiddle. It flick-flacked
through the air like a dumb and clumsy bird and,
though I heard the splash of its landing, I did not
care enough to mark if it floated or sank. The
bow followed. Then so did I.

I should have drowned that morning, Ja. The
pull of my clothes, and the weight of the rock I
had tied, like a widow's hump, to my back, should
have seen to it. That and the fact that I dived, face
down, into deep water and opened my mouth to
my drowning as eagerly as any fish to its continued
survival.

I should have died, and been left to bloat and
stink. Eels should have had me. Pike should have
nosed at my bones.

But as the lake poured itself into me . . . as my
chest and throat seemed fit to explode from the
weight . . . the surprising weight . . . of water . . .
I felt myself being rolled and tugged . . . drawn
by some sudden tide, or force, back towards
the shore.

I fought like a cat in a sack. I kicked and
flailed and battled to stay under—to finish what
I'd started and have done. Curses boiled in my
head, then bubbled from the gawp of my mouth,
as I reached with greedy fingers, for whatever
might hold me down. But no reeds would bind
me. No mud would grip my wrists. No stones
would be my anchor while I drowned.

The lake spat me out. It tossed me, face down, onto shingle and silt, gave my heels a smack and then retreated. The rock on my back fell away, and I raised my sorry face a few inches from the ground as all that I had swallowed came spewing back out. Right, I thought. I'll try again. Only with poison this time. With Deadly Nightshade—the Devil's cherries. And, for good measure, I'll open my wrists.

'Look up.'

I heard the command and shook my head. Not in rebellion but because I believed my ears to be full, still, of lake water. How else to explain the booming of that dreadful and all too familiar voice outside my head instead of in it? Up on my hands and knees I was by then, Ja, shaking that head of mine like a crazed dog and thinking: wrong time of year for the nightshade berry, so maybe throat as well as wrists?

'Look up, Jack Orion.'

I was beyond being afraid. I was beyond all sense and feeling; so I turned my head, without care or curiosity, and looked.

The figure glaring down at me wore a cowl, like a holey man, although as I was soon to understand, and the saints have always known, he has never been a monk—just a master of disguise. He had a beard, such as a goat might sport, and red in the whites of his eyes.

I knew him, in an instant, for the cove who had once owned my fiddle. And though we had never met before—except vaguely, in a dream—I felt a kinship with him that made my empty stomach heave, and heave again, so unexpected was this bolt of recognition and so . . . awful.

## 'Pull yourself together, you mewling little puke. And listen, well, to what I have to say.'

My stomach gave a final heave. 'Go on then,' I managed. 'Speak your piece.' I would not look at him again. I kept my eyes on the patch of ground between my hands—on the wet slop I had made of it—as he said what he had come to say:

## 'Go back to London, Jack Orion, for there is much more, there, to do.'

I'd sooner die, I replied. And I will, too, before this day is out.

At that he laughed. A real belly laugh, Ja; so ordinary—so merry—that I would have swivelled round, to see what tickled him so, had

I not been set on remaining absolutely still. Then he prodded me in the ribs, and it hurt.

'The moment and manner of your passing my sweet, is not for you to decide,' he said. 'It rests with me. Always has, and always will. For you are my son, in whom I am rather pleased.'

The day darkened for me, then, Ja. Or maybe it didn't. Maybe it was my own sight that dimmed, so that I could no longer see the ground. I could not move. I could not think. I just stayed there, on my hands and knees, and had he turned me, then, into a boulder, for water birds to crap on and the lake to slosh over and around, for ever and a day, it would have been a mercy.

But he doesn't deal in mercy. That is not what he is about.

I have the Devil's luck, Ja and his rude health, to boot. I can turn living things to stone, if I want to badly enough. And now I know why.

The bad thoughts that have plagued me, for as long as I can recall, were never truly mine. It was him, giving me guidance. Teaching me how to be. Isn't that what fathers do?

*I am Jack Orion. Jack the Lad, as was. I am the Devil's spawn and my heart could break from knowing.*

It is early morning; the sun barely risen. The stonemason moves, quickly, through the grounds of Orion House. He can smell the roses that ramble, untamed, up and over high stone walls. The scent, at this hour, is pleasant. Later, as the sun warms and then scorches the flowers, it will be cloying. A sick, sweet, stench.

The steps leading up to Orion House need sweeping. Cobwebs drape the fine front door, and the two wooden 'J's, intertwined, have been made filthy by the starlings that shelter under, and between, the letters' curves.

The door, the stonemason knows, will be bolted. Should he knock, he will get no reply. But he never knocks. Why would he? In the fifteen months of his coming here, once or twice a week, he has crossed paths with Jack Orion only a handful of times: twice on the steps, once in the cloister, and once in the rose garden, where the boy had gone to weep.

Hoping, as always, to come and go unseen, the stonemason climbs the steps. On the top one is a basket, empty except for crumbs. Slipping a bag from his shoulder, the stonemason transfers a loaf, a cheese, a fish, cooked and wrapped, a punnet of berries and a flagon of ale from bag to basket, and covers the lot with a rough wooden lid.

'Your provisions are here,' he calls out. 'And your goats are well.' Starlings wheel, alarmed, from the wooden 'J's, but no reply comes from behind the closed door. It never does.

Job done, the stonemason hurries away. He will see to the goats next.

Cutting through the rose garden, he quickens his pace. Finding Orion there, that one time—almost a year ago now—had surprised and unsettled him. He hadn't known what to do; had merely shifted from one foot to the other and held fast to the bag of provisions until the boy, sensing his presence, had spun round, his face tortured, a howl caught in his throat.

'Food,' the stonemason had ventured, holding up the bag. 'And your goats are well.'

Orion had shaken his head, befuddled, and stared, wildly, up at the sky. 'I miss her,' he had croaked. 'It's unbearable.'

'Ah . . .' The stonemason had trawled his memory for a name, or some other clue, but the names and faces of the vanished had faded, quickly, for him. He knew them better as stones. 'Who . . . which one?' he had faltered.

'Janet.' Pleasure and pain had taken turns on Jack Orion's face, as he savoured the sound of that name. 'Janet. Janet Huckle. It was she, not the sister, who married Sam Huckle's apprentice. You got that wrong, dolt.'

'Ah,' the stonemason had repeated. 'The bride stone.'

Jack Orion had whirled round, fast. 'You know which one she is?' he had cried out. 'You *know?*'

'Well—yes.'

'Then tell me. *Tell me!*'

And so, the stonemason had told him.

Hurrying, now, past the spot where Orion had hugged him—hugged and lifted him clean off his feet—he blushes to recall how he had squawked like a chicken, in surprise and alarm, and begged to be set down.

Since then, he knows, Orion has been seen flitting past the church, long after dark, on his way to visit the stones. Men stumbling from the tavern have called out to him, 'Go well, sir. God grant you rest,' but have neither expected nor received a reply. Folk hereabouts (the few who dared remain) know only that Jack Orion shuns all human company and is no longer quite right in his head. Rumour has it that he was in love with Alice Bundy and that grief over the way she went has made him solitary and strange. The stonemason keeps his own counsel. Alice. Janet. It hardly matters now.

Astonishingly little has been done, or said, about the appearance of the stones; perhaps because whole families went together, leaving no spouse, child or parent to cry out for justice or revenge. The priest packed up and left, scared witless by such diabolical doings on his doorstep. The tavern keeper, and others who remained, are in such deep shock, still, that it borders on denial. 'They be afeared to talk of it,' the stonemason told Jack, during their first, brief, encounter on the steps of Orion House. 'Lest the Devil overhears, and turns them solid, too.'

The stonemason does not regret telling Jack the exact shape and position of the bride stone. But he has no wish to discuss the matter further, with Orion or anyone else. When the stones first appeared, he found them fascinating—couldn't leave them alone. 'Stay away,' the old priest had warned, before he upped and left. The stonemason had not heeded his advice. Unafraid, he had spent many hours sitting or walking among the stones, noting their differences; checking for clues.

Each stone, he is quite certain, is solid right through. No cavities containing flesh and bone. No lost souls hammering for release. Still, in those early days, he was aware of certain vibrations. A hum, barely audible, emanating from each stone. These faint sounds enabled him to work out who each stone had been. Not by name—he couldn't have managed that—but by character, or profession.

The carpenter. The midwife. The lamed gossip. The bride.

A tavern girl. A tavern boy. The girl who could not see.

Within days, the vibrations had faded, never to return. The stonemason no longer visits the meadow or thinks, much, about the stones. He has no one to mourn, after all—unlike Jack Orion—and tending Orion's goats keeps him busy. He had never thought to be a goatherd, but finds he enjoys the change. Working with stone, he has concluded, can harden a man to a worrying degree. People still unnerve him, but the goats have become his friends.

'My goats!' he calls, as he leaps towards the herd. 'My girls and boys!' and the welcoming bleats he hears, in reply, are enough to warm his heart.

*Sorry. I've been asleep. Dead to the world (or as close to that state as I can ever expect to be). Re-living my encounter by the lake . . . imagining you, reeling away from me because of who and what I am . . . well, it made me sick at heart, Ja, and, suddenly, very tired.*

*The trouble, though, with having slept all afternoon, then right through the night, is that here I am again, wide awake at noon. And, in daylight, Ja. I cannot help but think of you.*

*The stonemason has been, with my provisions. He comes often—we have an arrangement—but I rarely know the hour. Would I starve without him? To death, I mean? Probably not. He has brought for me a fish this time. Berries too, so I'm guessing it's June or July.*

*I am sitting at my table. There is room at it
for thirty. Never once, though, in all this time,
has anyone joined me here. Except . . . but I'll
come to that.*

*I could be more sociable, had I the heart for
it. I could invite the neighbours in. After all, no
one has ever blamed me for what happened. I
am above suspicion. Around here they believe it
was the Devil himself who turned your wedding
party to stone. For dancing on the Sabbath, no
less! And, if you think about it, Ja, they are right.
Not about the dancing, but about who, exactly,
was to blame.*

*Wretched boy! I hear you say. 'Twas you
who played the fiddle, and you who wished us
ill. Well, yes. I can't argue with that. But don't
you see? He was in my head, Ja, twisting me to
his will. He'd been doing it all my life and I
didn't know.*

*I tell you what, though—and this is
important—I don't hear him any more. I keep
expecting to. It's one reason why I sleep a lot—
he never got to me, in sleep, except the once, at
court. I'm tempting fate, I know, just daring to
think myself free. Free to be anything I want,
including good.*

*But there, I've just touched wood, for good luck
and protection. And very fine wood it is too. Did
your father fashion this table, or did the holey*

men leave it behind? I might ask the stonemason about that, next time we meet. He'll know.

I feel safe at this table, Ja. At peace, almost. But let's go back to the lake. I want you to know what happened, after I met my father.

I have no idea how long I stayed, crouched like a beast upon the shore, and waiting for something to happen. Eventually, I became aware that my wrists and knees were aching and I was chilled, right to the bone. With the aches and the chill came a sudden rush of thoughts. My own, mercifully.

I thought of you. I thought of rain hitting, and bouncing off stone, and of snow piling up around what used to be your knees. And I told myself that no suffering of mine, from that day on, could ever be too great.

I forced myself to move. To sit back on my heels and get my bearings. The shore appeared deserted; the lake calm. By the play of light on water, and the position of the sun, I guessed it to be noon, or thereabouts.

I did not trust him to be gone.

A water bird wheeling overhead, eyed me, as it passed. There was spite in its regard. Was it him? Or there . . . there in the distance; at the farthest point of the lake . . . was that him, fading to grey in his borrowed robes? I blinked. The shape shifted and was gone.

*I stood up.*

*A breeze ruffled my hair, as if attempting to dry it for me. Was that him? 'Don't touch me!' I yelled, shrugging my wet shirt up over my head, in case it was. 'And don't trouble me again. I . . . I disown you. Do you hear?'*

*I waited, shivering, for his response. For a roar between my ears, or another smack from the lake. For a tremor underground or the smell of something burned.*

*Nothing.*

*'**Do you hear me?**' I hollered again, my voice scraping my throat.*

*Still nothing.*

*And, you know what, Ja, that wounded me. To my eternal shame I found his silence harder to bear, at that moment, than anything else he might have done. I felt myself an abandoned child; a child left to shiver, and fend for itself, until its parent sees fit to reappear and tell it what to do.*

*I staggered away from the lake and up onto the lane. My wet clothes steamed in the sun. I wondered, vaguely, where my hat was.*

*Where to go? What to do?*

*I yearned to go home, but where was 'home', for me, if not with you? With the living, breathing, you, I mean. **In Hell,** came the obvious answer, dropped like a hot coal into*

my head. And I could not bear it. Could. No
Longer. Endure.

Too weak to run, I made myself walk. At
some point, I crawled; and with the crawling
came the babbling and a pitiful desire to be
picked up, cradled and soothed. After I know
not how long a time; I arrived, bleeding, at
your father's house. And so deranged was I, by
then, that it was no longer you I longed for, as
I pushed the gate open and crawled along the
path. It was my mother.

You owned a lot of handkerchiefs, you Huckles.
To this day, I am not sure, if the one I took
away was my mother's. Each of yours had a
little 'J' stitched, in green, in one corner; your
sister's very large 'D's; but there were others
in the linen chest with no stitching on at all.
I handled them carefully, with my grazed and
filthy fingers. The coarse workaday ones, I
guessed to be your father's. But what of the
remaining four?

The thought of taking one of Annie's old snot
rags by mistake made me squirm. But surely, I
thought, you would have kept my own mother's
parting gift to me separate from the rest? And
the ring? I had forgotten, until that moment,
about the ring. And so I asked myself: where
might your conniving hedgewitch of a mother

have put my inheritance, if not upon your finger, where it belonged?

Slam went the lid of the chest, and off I went a-looking.

There was no need—I can admit it now—to have smashed every pot and cup in your mother's kitchen; or to have torn all your wedding flowers down and stamped upon their heads. Nor was it strictly necessary for me to have ripped your bedding apart with my teeth, or to have hacked at the table, with your father's axe, until it splintered, groaned and swayed.

I could have searched methodically, taking care to put stuff back. I could have shown more respect for your family's things. But forgive me, Ja, I was in no mood to be neat.

Your cat came in, halfway through this rampage, but turned tail straightaway and fled. I have no idea what became of it, but don't fret. Cats are clever. It would have fended for itself well enough, in the woods or by the lake. Still is, for all I know.

It may have been the cat coming in; or perhaps I just lost heart, but I dropped the axe, while the table still stood, and went back to the linen chest.

The ring, I had to accept, was nowhere to be found. It struck me, then, that your mother might have sold it, to pay for your wedding feast.

I could imagine the pleasure that would have given her, and it made my blood boil.

My blood. There was more of it, now, coming from one of the deeper cuts on my left palm. I used a handkerchief of yours to staunch the flow—such a small connection to you, Ja, but it gave me some comfort to press that green 'J' to my wounds while I tried once again to identify my property.

Speak to me, I willed the four unmarked handkerchiefs. And it did not seem mad to ask it, or to expect a reply. Not after the morning I'd had.

In the end, though, I had to decide. All four possibles were white, but only two had borders of lace. My mother was a lady. She would have had lace on everything. Of the two lace-trimmed possibles, one had a sorrier look, as if long-stored, and a staining in the centre that no amount of washing had removed. I took that one. It felt right. I put all the others back in the chest, including the one with your initial, and my blood on it.

Then I left your father's house, taking only what was mine.

And so I stepped, for the first time, into Orion House. The key was where I had left it; everything inside just so. Do you want me to describe the place? Do you really want that, Ja? Will it comfort you to know that the hangings are sumptuous, the view from the top floor entrancing and the bed easily as fine as the King's own? And that none of these things have ever given me solace, or a single moment's pleasure? Well know it, if you must, and be glad.

So exhausted was I that I noticed not the hangings, or anticipated the view, as I staggered across the hall towards the stairs. I needed sleep—longed for it—but: not on the bed, I told myself. Not without her. Don't go up those stairs, Jack Orion, to fall upon the bed, for it will break your sorry heart to have to lie there all alone.

There is a chair at the head of my table: a rare and handsome piece, not unlike a throne. I'm sitting on it now. Set high into the opposite wall, directly above the table's end is a window shaped like an arch. When the holey men were here there was a picture in that arch, made of brightly coloured glass. It showed Our Lady cradling her newborn son; the magi looking on; a host of angels looking down. Our Lady's robes were the colour of bluebells and her halo, when the sun shone through, a blaze of perfect glory. The King's men smashed this scene to pieces. The new glass—my glass—is plain, showing only sky, and the occasional star, distorted.

*I knew nothing about the original window, or the tales connected to it, when first I stumbled into this house. The stonemason told me later, when we crossed paths in the cloister. All I knew, as I collapsed into my chair—collapsed all a-sprawl, as if shot from the mouth of a cannon—was that my life was over. That being unable to end it properly, with poison or water or rope was neither here nor there.*

*This state I'm in, I thought, is a sort of living death. For I cannot move. I cannot be. I am in Hell, already. It is done.*

*I bent forward, then, weary beyond all measure, and let my head rest on the table's top. I thought of Katherine Howard—of the way she had placed herself, just so, for the axe. I'm sorry, I thought, closing my eyes. Majesty. Dancing girl. I can say it now, and mean it. I am so, so sorry.*

*How strange it felt, this sorriness, and how new. It washed through me, as sweet as you like and, Ja, I fought it not.*

*I thought of the Old Man. Of how I never said goodbye to him, or thank you, Old Man, for raising me—ill-tempered little whelp that I was. Sorry Scratch, I thought. Sorry, Old Man.*

*I thought of Thomas Culpeper . . . of Sam, your father . . . of your sister, and your mother, and of all those wedding guests. Sorry, sorry, sorry. I thought until the word seemed as much* a part of me as the cuts upon my palms and the darkness in my heart.

I thought, then, of Brother Day. And the 'sorry' that had half-formed itself, and was waiting for its turn, quivered in my head, and backed away.

It might have vanished altogether, that half-formed sorry. It might have fizzled out completely, with a hiss. For as heat began to line my skull I knew that my father was with me, still, determined to be heard.

I clenched my fists. My mother's handkerchief was all balled up in one of them. She was only human, Old Scratch said before he died. And so she was, and so, in part, am I.

I clung to that knowledge. I clung to it as fiercely as I clung to the handkerchief. And, though the heat in my head had grown close to intolerable I forced myself—my human self—to think, again, about Thomas Day. Your husband.

Thomas and Janet Day. Man and wife. Tom and Jannie, in love with one another, for ever and a day. A 'T' and a 'J' entwined. Two sparrows in a nest. What sweet-tempered children they would have had and known. What contentment.

Forgive me, I whispered. Both of you. For I am truly sorry.

It was then I felt the touch of something, cool upon my head. I wanted to look up, but could not.

*For my mind—that poor, damaged place—had*
*begun a-boiling and a-seething like never before.*
*So many words . . . so many filthy words . . . and*
*sounds . . . and threats . . . and visions.*

*My head was a mire, Ja. A place of sin*
*and shame. Had it split, I do believe, all Hell*
*would have been let loose upon the table. Bile*
*and vipers. Spikes and screams. A cascade of*
*burning hearts,*

*And then it stopped. Not suddenly, but in a*
*slow, steady way, like a tide going out. I felt him*
*leave. I swear, I felt him go. And then it was just*
*me, sprawled face down on the table; my mind*
*an empty room with a breeze blowing through.*

*And whatever had touched, and cooled, the*
*crown of my poor head was still there.*

*I raised my face, a fraction, opened my eyes and*
*looked. And there it was—the shadow of some*
*kind of a pole, stretching the whole length of the*
*table's top and, less than a foot from my nose, the*
*shade of another, shorter, pole, going cross-ways.*

*A cross.*

*I was in the shadow of a cross.*

*The voice, when it came, was both in and all*
*around me.*

CHILD.

BE STILL.

*I had heard that voice, and those very words,*
*before. In the bluebell wood, that day we found*

226

*each other. They had slipped into my head, from
I knew not where, and banished some terrible
thoughts. I should have paid more heed to that
voice. I should have listened, hard, for it later on, or
willed it to return. I listened this time, though. This
time, I let those words sink into me, like balm.*

*I felt picked up, cradled and soothed. I felt
forgiven, Ja. And blessed.*

*When the cross began to fade I jolted forward
in my chair; stretched out a dirty hand and let it
tremble over the table; not daring to touch the
shadow, as it went, only yearning with all my
sorry heart for it to stay.*

*But you know what, Ja? I think it did stay,
although I see it not. I'll be alone at this table,
eating my bread, or drinking my ale, and I'll
get that soft, cool feeling again as if a kindly
hand rests upon my head, letting me know—
reminding me—that I have nothing more to fear
in this house . . . this world . . . this life.*

*So that's everything. That's all that has
happened to me since your wedding day. It has
done me a wealth of good to tell you, if only in
my mind. Indeed, I feel almost cheerful. Being
awake during the day is not, perhaps, so terrible.
I might do it again, on purpose.*

*Now—how might we amuse ourselves, before
I seek some rest? Sometimes, Ja, I look up at my*

arched window and imagine my own nativity there. Let's do it together; I'd like that.

I was born in a goat shed, so first we'll add some goats: Mollykins, Lavender, Trot. They can go where I'm guessing the magi were in that other, far holier, scene. Now picture, if you will, my mother. No halo for her, I'm afraid, and her face, though lovely, is not exactly glad. I'm naked, in her arms, and I am screaming. The man who was not my father ought, I suppose, to be standing at my mother's side. Let's do him in muted colours, so that he's barely there at all.

Now we'll add the Devil. Shall we give to him horns and a tail? Or should he be as I imagine he was when he beguiled my mother? Dark-haired and handsome, like me. All right. Horns and a tail it is. He must go above my mother and I in shades of red and orange. He must blaze there for a moment, glaring down with dreadful eyes, and you and I must stare right back, to show we do not care.

Now we can smash that picture up. Just by thinking it—we don't need rocks, or poles— we can send it crashing outwards, leaving just the sky.

There.

It is accomplished.

Doesn't that feel good?

* * *

'Ah . . .' The stonemason stops dead in his tracks. *Not again*, he thinks. *I can't cope, again, with his wailings and lamentations.* From now on, he decides, he will take a different route to the steps of Orion House. The rose garden will soon be impassable anyway; the paths crossed and hung all about by thorns.

At least, he observes, Orion is decently attired this time. Before, he was barefoot, and wearing only a nightshirt. And he's not crying, thanks be. He is . . . well . . . he is picking a bunch of roses.

If he keeps quiet, the stonemason thinks, he might just be able to slip past . . .

'Mason!' Jack turns and waves. He looks pleased, the stonemason notes. He looks . . . normal. He has found gloves from somewhere, to protect his hands from thorns, and a wooden trug in which the flowers he has already picked lie, long-stemmed and lovely.

'Sir. I . . . um . . . I have your provisions, and your goats are well.'

'Do you? Are they? Jolly good.'

Jack removes his gloves. He is smiling as he bounds towards the stonemason, his right hand outstretched. The stonemason backs away. *No hugs*, he thinks. *Please.*

But Orion only wants to shake his hand. To thank him, most heartily, for all that he has done, these past fifteen months, and for all that he will continue to do, if he pleases, for Orion has no wish to hire a cook, or any other servants, with their prying eyes and clacking tongues. And he himself had never cut the mustard as a goatherd. Not really.

'You look well, sir,' the stonemason says, when Orion finally stops for breath. What he means to say is thank you; I will serve you all my days, for it is a life that suits me well, and I . . . I cut the mustard nicely, as a goatherd.

'I feel well,' Orion tells him. 'I feel very well indeed. But, then, so I should.'

The stonemason has no answer to that. He nods, looking blank.

'Do you remember, Mason,' Orion continues, 'when I asked you, that time in the cloister, about the shadow on my table? And you told me you had seen it too, although it touched you not?'

'I remember.'

'Well, then . . .' Jack Orion beams. And the stonemason, who has carved and chiselled nothing for more than a year, wishes, momentarily, for the materials, and the skill, to capture such radiance . . . such dark beauty . . . for all time.

'. . . it touched me,' Orion says. 'I didn't tell you that. I haven't told anyone, except my Ja. It's taken a while, I'll admit, for me to feel this blessed. For me to trust, and believe, in what occurred. But better late than never, eh, Mason?'

'Indeed,' the stonemason says.

'So what's in the bag?' Orion asks.

230

'The bag? Oh. A loaf, sir. And more berries. And a cheese I made myself. A goat's cheese, well-wrapped so it will keep.'

'Excellent,' says Orion, clapping him on the back. 'Leave it by the door, as usual. I'm going for a stroll.'

The stonemason watches, as Orion collects his trug of blood-red roses and strides, whistling, away. It is not hard to guess where the boy is headed.

Shadows and stones. Crosses and thorns. Can a shadow bless? Can a stone hum? Was it truly the Devil himself who . . . ? It is all a mystery to the stonemason and he is content to leave it so.

*I should have done this sooner—come to you in daylight, that is. No one was stopping me. There have been no mobs outside my gates, hurling abuse, or salt, or dung. No guards sent by His Majesty to escort me to the Tower. I suppose I just needed time. To grieve. To adjust.*

*I wore the night, I suppose, like an extra cloak, to cover and hide my shame.*

*Still, I'm here now.*

*Hello.*

*I've brought roses. Red ones from my garden. They smell heavenly, do they not? I thought, on the way here, about planting some at your feet, but I don't want you scratched, or bothered by bees.*

*I'm going to sit down, as close to you as*

*I can get. And, yes, I'm turning my back on
your husband but I mean nothing by it. No
disrespect.*

*It's actually rather lovely up here, Ja. I'd
forgotten how lovely it can be. I'm glad for
you that the view today is clear and the air so
deliciously warm. At night, even in summer, I've
sat here and worried that you might be cold. More
than once—don't laugh—I've been tempted to
throw a blanket over you, or wrap you all around
in furs, the way I'd intended to do, on winter days,
had things gone the way they should.*

*Jack the Lad, I hear you say, you are too kind.
Hah!*

*See that thrush, sharpening its beak on that
stone over there? Whose head is that? Your
mother's? I'm sorry, I shouldn't smirk. Hang on,
I'll shoo it away.*

*There.*

*It's gone.*

*If it comes anywhere near you, I'll catch it and
snap its neck. No. I'm joking. I don't do those
things any more.*

*How blue the sky is this afternoon. As blue
as your eyes. And can you feel the sun, as I do? I
would touch you, Ja, but I don't know where your
hand is and would not want to get that wrong.*

*You know what? I'm almost happy. And why
should I not be so? What happened to you was*

dreadful. A tragedy. A crime. But it wasn't my fault.
I didn't plan it. It wasn't my fault. It wasn't.

You do forgive me, don't you? You ought to,
you know. I've been cleansed, after all—blessed
by the Holey Cross—and you don't get more
forgiven than that.

I'm not the bad Ja any more. I'm just your
Jack the Lad. Jack Orion if you must.

An ordinary boy with ordinary thoughts.

# And so much, still, to tell you.

# *Author's Note*

In a field, in rural Somerset, stand the stones of Stanton Drew. Nobody knows for sure why they are there. To be alone among them is spooky, particularly if the light is fading. Then, they loom like elephants and you feel you ought to run. The ones that have toppled seem merely to be resting. 'Sorry,' you want to say to them. And 'No, no—don't get up.'

Legend has it that these mysterious stones were people, once—a wedding party, of some thirty souls, dancing and making merry. When the church clock struck midnight, they should have stopped. They should have caught their breaths, sobered up, and gone home to their beds. But they didn't.

'We'll play no more,' the musicians cried. 'For 'tis the Sabbath now, and only the Devil's children do dance on the Sabbath Day.'

But the newlyweds and their guests would not be told. They were having too much fun. And when a handsome dark-haired stranger stepped forward, offering to play the fiddle, they hurrahed and cheered him on.

The Devil smiled as he raised his bow, and the tune he fiddled was wild. Faster he played, and faster still, and, as the wedding party whirled and skipped, he turned them all to stone.

This story inspired **DANCE of the DARK HEART**, but only loosely. I went off on a tangent, I got carried away. But that's the good thing about re-imagining a legend: nothing is set in stone.

Julie Hearn
Oxford
Spring, 2013

Also by Julie Hearn,

The Merrybegot

Turn the page for a taster of what's in store . . .

## The Confession of Patience Madden
## The Year of Our Lord, 1692

Good day, brothers. I am ready to talk to you now. Ready to tell you the truth. Pray forgive the croak in my voice. It has been . . . it has been . . .

Water? Yes. Thank you . . .

Are you listening? I can barely see you. It is so dark in here . . .

Are you ready?

Then I will begin.

I never meant it to end the way it did. Grace might have done, but not me. Grace was fifteen, as artful as a snake, and already on the slippery slope to Hell. But I, Patience Madden, could have stopped any time—uncrossed my eyes; made my arms and legs be still; and called a halt to the filthy words jumping out of my mouth like toads. I could have spat the pins from under my tongue and admitted they came not from the Devil but from the cherrywood box our mother kept tiny things in.

I could have sat up in bed, looked around at the villagers come to whisper and gawp, and said No. Stop praying for me. Stop bringing me bay leaves and splashes of holy water. For I don't deserve your lucky charms, nor any help from the Lord. Neither does my sister. She deserves them even less. It was her fault. She started it. And now she's hurting me. Yes, she is. Pinching me black and blue beneath the coverlet, lest I weaken and tell you the truth.

*Grace, I whispered, on the third evening, after our neighbours had drifted away to feed their hogs, their children, or their own nosy faces. Grace, I'm scared. I want to get up. Grace, I'm hungry.*

*Be silent, she hissed. Or, if you can't be silent, call out some more about imps at the window, and a crow in the corner. That was good. They liked that. We'll do more with the imps and the crow.*

*She promised me I would not have to behave like this for much longer. In a day or so, she said, we would stage our recovery. Wake up all smiles, ready to put on our itchy bonnets, and do our tiresome chores, like good, obedient girls.*

*A few days more, she said, and our lives would go back to normal. As dull as scum, but blameless.*

*It did not happen like that. It went too far.*

*We went too far.*

# April 1645

The cunning woman's granddaughter is chasing a pig when she learns there is to be no frolicking in the village on May morning. Minister's orders.

'Bogger . . . that,' she pants. 'And bogger . . . this . . . pig. There's no . . . catching . . . him . . .'

Clutching her sides, she gives up the chase, and collapses, laughing, against the gnarled trunk of a tree. Above her head, pink blossoms shake like fairy fists. Spring has arrived. A beautiful time. A time when it feels absolutely right to think of dancing barefoot in the dew, and absolutely wrong to dwell on the new minister, with his miserable ways and face like a trodden parsnip.

'That's what they be saying,' the blacksmith's son tells her. 'No pole. No goin' off into the woods. No nothing. It ain't godly, Nell, to frolic so. That's what the minister reckons.'

Nell picks a blade of new grass and begins to chew it. Her stomach rumbles beneath her pinafore, but she is used to that. Out of the corner of her eye she can see the pig rooting around. It is a bad pig. A bothersome pig. Her granny will sort it out. This is how:

# A Spell to Soothe a Truculent Pig

*First, catch your pig. Do it on a Monday, on a waning moon, when the time be right for healing. Point him to the north, and hang on tight.*

*Rap his snout three times with a wand of oak, and call: 'Powers of earth, tame and soothe this creature that he may become docile and no longer a bogging nuisance.'*

*Wait seven beats of the heart, then let him go.*

*So mote it be.*

A light breeze frisks the orchard. There are things Nell ought to be doing, but she stays where she is, squinting up at the blacksmith's son and thinking about May morning.

'And who be you wishing to frolic with anyway, Sam Towser?' she chuckles. 'As if I couldn't guess . . .'

The lad reddens. He is a month short of sixteen and all swept through with the kind of longings that can tie up a boy's tongue and have him tripping over everything, from clods of earth to his own great feet, twenty times a day. He has a mop of corn-coloured hair, and a cleft in his chin so deep it might have been pressed there by his guardian angel. He is too ungainly; too unfledged, as yet, to be truly handsome. But he will be. The promise of it is all about him, like the guarantee of a glorious day once some mist has cleared.

'No one,' he mumbles. 'I got horses to see to. No time for fumblin' around with some daft maid on May mornin', nor any other time.'

'Pah! That's a fib!' Nell flings both arms wide and twists her face to look like a parsnip. 'Beware, sinner! Beware what you say! Repent! Repent! For Satan loves a fibber, and will carry you off to burn in Hell. In Hell, I tell you, where fibbers go. And frolickers. And women who wear scarlet ribbons, or sweep their hearths on Sundays . . .'

'Hush . . . Hush up, you daft wench . . .'

'Repent! Repent! For I am your minister. God's representative in this heathen place . . . Repent! For though my nose drips and I do not know a hoe from my . . .'

'NELL, hush!'

'. . . elbow, I know a sinner when I see one. And a fibber. And a frolicker. All rolled into one vile, wretched . . .'

'Right!'

'. . . body . . . and a . . . Yieeek! . . .'

He has pounced and is tickling her—tickling her to what feels like a giggly death, while the sun pours down like honey, and the truculent pig looks on in mild surprise.

'You two! Have a care! Mind that tree, and stop your messing.'

A woman has entered the orchard. She stands some distance away, almost in the nettles. Her face, beneath a bonnet the colour of porridge, is grave.

'What?' Nell scrambles to her feet. 'What is it, Mistress Denby? What's happened?'

The blacksmith's son gets up. There are twigs and fallen

petals in his hair. He looks like Puck. He looks drop-dead frolicsome.

'Gotter go,' he mutters. 'I got horses to see to.'

The woman and the girl pay him no mind. They have already jumped the stile and are hurrying away, along the crooked path leading down to the village. Women's stuff, he supposes. Someone getting born. Or dying. Or doing both in the space of a few breaths.

He doesn't want to be seen trotting at the heels of womenfolk, towards whatever, or whoever, needs their attention in some fusty room. The sun is high, now, and he has his own ritual to perform.

The apple tree he chooses is truly ancient; its timber as knotted as a crone's shins; its blossom strangely pale. No one knows how long it has stood here, or why it was planted alone. Much older than the rest, it continues to bear fruit so sweet that to press cider from it, and drink the stuff, is said to send the mind dribbling out of the nostrils and the legs in several directions at once.

It is to this tree the Apple Howlers come, on Twelfth Night, to scare away evil spirits. It is here that they form their circle—a raggle taggle of villagers, young and old, banging pails and pots and howling, *'Hats full! Caps full! Bushels, bushels, sacks full!'* loud enough to wake the dead.

It is on these branches, and around this trunk, that the Howlers hang their amulets and leave cider-soaked toast for the piskies. The orchard swarms with piskies. Everyone knows that. Little folk in rags, their skin as rough as bark, their heads sprouting lichens and moss. A few are down-right malicious, the rest merely troublesome and high-spirited. All are uglier than dead hedgehogs and as greedy as swine. Over the hills, in a neighbouring county, lies fairy territory—a prettier species, by far, the fairies, but just as pesky, so rumour has it . . . just as demanding of treats, and remembrance.

Be good to the piskies, the old folk say hereabouts, and they will be good to you. Treat them with respect on Twelfth Night and they will stay by the trees, watching over the fruit until picking time comes.

The cider-soaked toast has been eaten long ago by robins and other things. But the amulets are still here, swaying gently at the end of their strings, like small, hanged felons.

'May I?' says the blacksmith's son, before pressing the point of a horseshoe nail into the old tree's trunk.

*Yep*, something replies, the sound of it such a faint rasp that the blacksmith's son assumes the pig has farted.

Slowly, carefully, he begins to cut. Not his full name—Samuel—for he isn't sure of all the letters. A single 'S' is the mark he makes, the down stroke wobbly as a caterpillar against the wood. He can't spell the other name, either. The one that is on his mind day and night. The one he only has to hear, in passing, for a fluttering to start in his belly, as if larks are nesting there.

He knows his alphabet though. Just. And he knows, from the way the girl's name is said, which letter he needs to entwine with his own. It is one of the tricky ones that sounds different, depending on the word. As the metal point of the nail forms the letter's curve he finds himself wishing it made a soft sound like the beginning of 'gentle'. He would have liked that. It would have seemed significant.

The girl's name, though, begins with a hard 'G', like 'gallows' or 'god'.

When he has finished, he steps back to inspect what he has done. And then he sees one. At least, he thinks he does. There and gone it is, between knots of blossom, its face as coarse and grey as the tree, its small, bright eyes fixed intently on the 'S' and the 'G'.

'Oh . . .'

He looks quickly, all around, and then back again. Nothing. There is nothing there. A trick of the light, perhaps? But no . . . His sight is good, and he isn't given to fancies.

He stays a minute more, half dreading, half hoping to see the thing again. What did it mean? Was it lucky, to see a piskie when you were a month short of sixteen and so desperate to get your hands on a certain someone that you would probably die of frustration if it didn't happen soon?

Did it mean that he would?

Did it?

It takes just seconds for the blacksmith's son to convince himself that he has been sent an auspicious sign. That, come May morning, he will be frolicking away to his heart's content with the girl whose name begins with a hard-sounding 'G'.

She will be all over him like a vine, yes she will, for all she is the minister's daughter and seems as distant and cool as a star. He will have her. No doubt about it. For they are joined, already, in his mind and on the tree. And their union has been blessed. He has the piskie's promise.

The blacksmith's son feels light on his feet as he swings himself over the stile, and he is whistling as he strides away.

'Silly young bogger . . .' goes the sighing and the rasping

among the topmost branches of the trees. *'Silly . . . little . . . whelp.'* And the letters 'S' and 'G' begin slowly turning brown, the way a cut apple will do, or naked flesh beneath hot sun.

Julie Hearn has been writing all her life. After training as a journalist, she went to Australia, where she worked on a daily tabloid newspaper.

She lived in Spain for a while before returning to England, where she worked as a features editor and freelance features writer.

After her daughter was born she went back to her studies and obtained a BA in English and a MSt in Women's Studies. She is now a full-time writer, and has been shortlisted for many awards including the Carnegie Medal, the Branford Boase Award, the Waterstones Book Prize, and the Guardian Children's Fiction Prize.